We can't all be sane all the time..

Amanda Jones is an upstanding citizen: mother, high school teacher, friend, and all around good citizen. Until the day she discovers herself bawling her eyes out in the emergency room. Who knew even normal people have breakdowns? Suicide, addiction, broken homes, relationship struggles, and learning to heal give Amanda plenty to think about as she documents her path of healing. At times funny and light, other times disturbingly real, Thirty Easy Days to Overcoming a Psychotic-Meltdown-Suicide-Scare-4-Year-Bender-Bi-Polar-Disaster-Session is a spirited look at our modern times and the path one woman follows to pull herself back from the brink. Follow Amanda as she digs herself out of her misery and learns how to once again find joy in life.

Thirty Easy Days to Overcoming a Psychotic-Meltdown-Suicide-Scare-4-Year-Bender-Bi-Polar-Disaster-Session

Megan McArther

Thirty Easy Days to Overcoming a Psychotic-Meltdown-Suicide-Scare-4-Year-Bender-Bi-Polar-Disaster-Session

This is a work of fiction. Names, characters, paces, and incidents either are the product of the author's imagination or are used fictionally.

For more information about Megan McArther visit our web page:
www.platformpublishers.com

Dedicated to Marla Regalado

Thirty Easy Days to Overcoming a Psychotic-Meltdown-Suicide-Scare-4-Year-Bender-Bi-Polar-Disaster-Session

Megan McArther

Day 1: The ER

The last Friday in January

My OB/Gyn asked how I was doing at my
yearly pap smear appointment. I'd had a rough
night, not able to sleep after my last class of the
day, ninth graders, declared mutiny. They were
led by an unmedicated kid with ODD/ADHD. The
principal and secretary rolled their eyes at my
inability to understand the discipline "procedure".
The stress and fatigue just got me down. My
general doctor hadn't been available for a week.

My psychiatrist couldn't see me for eleven more days.

How was I doing? Not great, I told her. My medication didn't seem to be working, and I was taking a ton of it. I'd been crying a lot, all the time it seemed for at least the last two weeks, about my ridiculously stresful job. After a couple more questions she asked if I'd thought about hurting myself.

"Yes," I admitted, "I've been thinking about taking all those pills right there, but I worried they wouldn't actually kill me. They would just make everything worse."

Her eyes widened as she snatched up all my meds, brushing them into her lab coat. The next thing I knew I was kindly escorted by Dr. McCleary to the Emergency Room as we made small talk about our children and the private school they all attend. For my sake we both tried to pretend this was a normal stroll through the hospital. She checked me in, and for one brief, glorious moment I thought my mental health crisis might finally be coming to a positive end. Maybe

I would finally get the treatment I needed. Not just more pills dumped on me with a pat on the head, advice to ignore the stressors that cause the issues, to just let the pills numb the pain. Endure.

Maybe I'd walk out of here all better! Like when I had my hernia repaired or when they sewed up my kid's knee or replaced my dad's hip.

But no. I was immediately thrust into a horrible, horrible damaging pit not at all suitable for a person in a crisis - right? Should someone who is freaking out, dripping tears and snot, a weepy mess, be stripped of their clothes and possessions, put into a windowless room and left alone? At first I refused to go in, afraid I'd be locked in, put into a straight jacket. I made the nurses reassure me multiple times that I would not be locked in or held prisoner. Should someone who is terrified and shaky and can't stop crying have to give up her clothes, have her purse and favorite purple hat from Italy and Famolare Heels taken away? The nurse seemed fairly trustworthy, but I hid my phone and a pen under a sheet, just in case. Plus I sneaked and didn't really take off all my clothes, I just pretended, tucking my black tank dress into the hospital pants pulling the cotton-y shirt over the top so no one could see. I might be crazy, but they couldn't make me look it. Then I watched as the CNA locked all my things into a safe while huddling under multiple warm blankets, alone on the hospital bed in the windowless room that could easily seal up and trap someone. I felt wronged for a moment. Until I realized my head no longer hurt. And I had stopped crying for the first time in I didn't know how long. Until the doctor - who I went to high school with (horrors!) and who's wife I socialize with (mortification!) came in. But he was compassionate. Professional. Helpful.

Maybe they do know what they are doing. I'm alive, huh? And I'm not thinking about 15-year-olds who do mean things to me and each other. No Stop. The pain returns.

How can I heal? Be still a moment. At least they recognize that I'm healthy enough to have a pen and a cell phone - oh wait, I hid those, they don't know. I could stab my eyes out with this pen. I could text psychotic things to people in the community. But for now I can write. And text my love and ask him to come get me.. Don't think of the world out there. It will be OK somehow. It will. Be well. Don't plan or scheme. Be well. Don't go back. Be well. Get medical leave. Be well. Heal. Be slow. Calm. Still. Train your brain to be calm. Pray. Calm.

Day 2: You're Headed Down the Same Path."

Saturday

I didn't drink or smoke ANYTHING!!!!! The doctors and I asked my love to take all my hidden medication stashes away. He gave me half doses of everything plus something called Lorazepam to help me with alcohol withdrawals. I slept a lot and ate a little and drank a ton of La Croix and cherry juice. I hugged and kissed my kids a lot.

Today I wade through, slow-motion, loosely stitched together, knowing the slightest disruption will tear me into shreds. The tears are further away, not quite so close to the surface. My head only hurts if I try to use my brain - math, or planning or remembering or harsh sounds or fears. Then the pain shoots back in.

I think of one thing the Crisis Counsellor said, as I described Maria and her surprising death. He asked, first, if I had a plan. I was embarrassed because all my suicide plans are dumb and poorly thought-out, like many of my plans in regular life, right? Like crashing into a semi, head-on, on the high way. But then I would just be a quadriplegic, a burden to others and unable to finish the job. Or, slightly more logical, to eat every one of my stock-piled pills, nice and neat, no mess to clean up. Except, like I told Dr. McCleary, it probably wouldn't really kill me, just make me all fucked up. Other dumb ideas: car on in the garage. Jumping off the Marcus Whitman. Dumb ideas, not thought through.

"But Maria, she hung herself," I told him.

He smacked his forehead.

"I know," I said, shaking my head, "unlike me she didn't just half-ass it. Buy how did she know what to do? How did she succeed? Buying the rope? What did she tie it to? Was she just drunk? Was it an accident?"

Here I pantomimed wrapping something around my own neck. "Maybe it was, maybe she was just drunk. The last time I talked to her, just a few days before she died, she told me she was drinking more than she'd ever drank in her life. Maybe she didn't mean to kill herself."

He looked at me with his calm, steady, Crisis-Counsellor eyes and said, "Amanda, you're headed down the same path."

I know. I know. I already know that people who, like Maria, have a parent commit suicide are something like 30% more likely to also commit suicide. I don't want this for my own kids. I also know I shouldn't drink and smoke pot while on psychotropic drugs. I am also aware that if I could get my mental health in order I could be amazing and successful and a wonderful example to my children and family. I know.

Day 3: Demolition Derby

Sunday

Tons of La Croix, cherry juice, a little food.
Lots of sleep. The right doses of pills.

First time in…I don't know, maybe five years,
that I've slept all night two nights in a row and I'm
not hung over nor am I drunk? Felt pretty good -
though still like I'd been kneaded into a pulpy
mass, just on the verge of tears. An article I wrote
a few months ago came out today in the
newspaper. The irony of it was not lost on me as I

read my cheerful words just days after melting down into a pile of nothing. I hope no one says anything to me about it. Or worse, asks when I'm going to write again. My editor has stopped even asking me if I have anything. I haven't really written in months. But seeing my cheery article in the lifestyles section of our local paper gave me a little kick in the pants. It is definitely time to get back on track.

Derby King!

Winston recently spent weeks preparing for the Roller Derby, finding the perfect outfit, choosing the right colors, the right wheels and decorations. We invited our family to come watch and everyone was all set and perfect - especially the car.

Wait. Wait. I mean, not Roller Derby....PINEWOOD Derby. Yes, Pinewood Derby. My 8-year-old son did not wear black eyeliner, ripped up stockings, a bustier, and a roller skates while knocking grown women to the floor in a brutal skating competition. No, I meant Pinewood Derby. Pinewood.

Winston is a Cub Scout. He designed a slick blue and green Dragster (Seahawks colors of course) complete with weighted pegs wedged into the back to make sure it met the 5-oz weight requirement. Winston, not being very adept at running a bandsaw or a drill, allowed Carlisle to help him a little. Oh, and he let Carlisle help with sanding too. And painting. And other minor engineering, little stuff. But Winston supervised.

The day of The Roller Derby - er, the Pinewood Derby - the dads gathered around the cars admiring their sons' work. The Cub Scouts, all decked out in their navy blue shirts and official yellow kerchiefs, checked out the dessert tables and played tag. The rest of us mingled, glad we didn't have to worry about creating little cars or race tracks.

As with all events involving large numbers of people, things took awhile to begin. The people who were wearing suits pulled out calculators and furrowed their brows over weights and numbers. The moms with babies fussed with feeding and diapers. The Scouts wrestled while singing Queen's 'We Will Rock You'. My dad talked about Jack Russell Terriers. I watched and wrote. The guys in suits continued to mull over numbers. No Scout would be going home with a trophy unless his car earned that trophy, by golly!

After the counting and measuring and careful notation the first heat began. The excitement! All the boys lined up on the floor along the track, eager to see their car win...soon to have their hopes dashed to disappointment as two particularly well-designed cars pulled ahead of the rest. Baker's streamlined white roadster and Daniel's shiny cut-out red car were far and away the superior vehicles.

What started out as an activity for learning about teamwork and craftsmanship now turned into a lesson on winning and losing with dignity. Winston struggled to contain his grief, excusing himself to cry alone outside. We let him be alone with his feelings for awhile, especially when he briefly tried to blame his chief engineer. He spent some more time alone at home, contemplating how he might apologize to his crew, eventually venturing out to talk to Carlisle and ask him to help him improve his design for next year. We finally got through to him about the power of good sportsmanship when we reminded him that his hero, Russell Wilson, always shakes hands with and congratulates the winner. I think Winston learned a good lesson that day.

In all, it was a good experience. Even if no one wore black eyeliner or ripped stockings.

Day 4: Cover the Crack Whore Nail Walls with Shiny Toilet Bowl Contact Paper

Monday

Alone today while kids were at school and my love was at work. Healthy, well rested, sober, and on the right medication thanks to my love and the fear of returning to windowless Emergency Room Crisis Center. I exercised at the YMCA for, oh, twenty minutes, doing the elliptical in slow motion surrounded by retirees. I listened to cheerful dance music and felt pretty good. Still flat and numb and terrified, but on my way somewhere other than down.

I went home and cleared out a bunch of crap, most notably from the garage area where I have liked to sneak out and smoke pot and cigarettes late at night after everyone is asleep. It was sunny and I opened both doors, letting the sun burn out the bad energy, reveling in the hope of newness and fresh beginnings. I swept and cleaned, blackening two rags with old ash and tobacco to the point where I just threw them in the garbage. In fact, once the garbage was full I just threw the whole can, avocado green and cracked clear up the side, into the big dumpster and walked away. Good riddance. I replaced my little roll-your-own cigarette system space in the cupboard with cleaning supplies, garden tools, and a pretty jeweled box full of colorful stones. Ha!! Take that bad habits.

Not to be too easily healed I spent the rest of the afternoon before picking kids up from school driving aimlessly around hoping for a new job or career to hit my windshield. I tithered around the Community College trying to meet up with different program directors to hear about other options (Electrician? Plumber? Heating and Cooling Installer? Landscape Architect?) but no one was available when I wanted to see them (meaning that instant) I ended up buying white contact paper at a big box store and covering up a hideous vine motif the previous owner of my house had painted in my kitchen. I liked this new look so much I started using the same white shiny contact paper to cover up the crack-whore scraped paint in the bathroom. Telling myself the central location of this bathroom was vital to my health, Feng-Shui-wise. Thinking it was urgent to immediately fix - even though I had been unsuccessful at getting this room remodeled for over a year. I left it half done. The shiny white contact paper looked like the bottom of the toilet had oozed out over the walls of the room. Better than crack-whore nail paint, though.

I drank a ton more sparkling water with cherry juice with a straw, becoming nearly as attached to this beverage/straw combo as I previously had been to a glass of wine. So there is that small victory. Slept for 14 hours.

Day 5: Hello again, Dr. Psychiatrist!

Tuesday

Sober. Now goes without saying. Must. Slept all night again. Could there, possibly, be a connection here? Hmmmm....profound thought of the day. Exercise. Lots of sparkling water with cherry juice.

I saw my psychiatrist today. He was very official, typing out my diagnosis, asking me

questions that I pretended not to struggle to answer
(What day is it? What year is it? Repeat these
words: green, can, Bill Clinton. What street are we
on? What is the name of the place we are in?
What were those three words?) He told me I can
be healthy without medication, yes!! But only if
I'm sober. Forever. yes. I know. I've always
known. We made a plan to make me better, wean
me off the drugs, some slowly, some immediately,
but all within three weeks. And psychotherapy.
And no work for now.

Best of all, a really good note for the school
saying I can return, but I only can teach in the
morning, the ninth graders, excusing me from the
biggest stressors. Yes!! Everyone needs a note
saying they can't work with hostile and aggressive
people, right?

That night was Groundhog Day. We went to
my dad's and had groundhog for dinner. (You
know, Ground Hog) It was wonderful. I was the
only one besides the kids who was not drinking
and I didn't miss it at all. I had my trusty La Croix
sparkling water and cherry juice (plus straw) and I

felt good. I wasn't drunk!!! What a lovely
surprise.

Day 6: 14 Emails from Work Induced Meltdown

Wednesday

I forgot to take my medication and then tried to exercise with my sister-in-law, but she isn't much of an exerciser. So no music and sweat today. Though I slept OK.

I ran around blindly again hoping a job would fall like a meteor onto my head, maybe knocking some sense into me, getting more and more upset about how I would return to work in three weeks. Were they laughing at me? Is that evil Stephanie secretary talking about me? Should I tell everyone she started dating her husband when she met him at church when he was sixteen and she was twenty-six? Do teachers at other schools know about me? Are the kids saying mean things? Are they saying they are glad I am gone? Will I get fired?

All of this induced by fourteen emails and four phone calls from ten different colleagues from the school Two subs (what do I do?), two kind teachers (are you ok?), the union president, a secretary (not the mean one), three administrators (where are you?), and a kid (one of my most difficult to work with students - "Where are you? We are tired of subs. Come back.") Plus two parents. Worst of all, I accidentally answered the phone one time and it happened to be my boss, just hearing her stern voice sent me into a tailspin and I ended up in child's pose on my living room floor. Sobbing. I thanked her for her compassion (I may have been a little facetious there) and got out of that phone hell, quick-like. I spent the rest of the morning crying until I realized I hadn't eaten or taken my half-doses of medication or had any of my trusty sparkling water with cherry (and straw). After taking care of my physical needs I lay down on the couch, turned on the Depak Chopra meditation experience (Success Comes From Within) and fell asleep for two hours. I slugged through the rest of the day, polite and caring to my kids of course. Going through the proper motions but secretly scared I'll never get better.

Day 7: Make No Decisions

Thursday

Remembering yesterday, I started the day off right. Drank a smoothie full of kambucha, plain yogurt, blueberries, a banana, spirulina, flax seed, turmeric, cocoa, bee pollen, and maca. Took the half pills. Exercised for an hour (slooooowly, while simultaneously updating my resume)

I cleaned and emptied my closets and took two full boxes to Goodwill, donating clothes that don't fit anymore (I think drinking 3500 calories worth of wine a week added to three different psychotic meds MAY have caused me to gain twenty pounds in the past six months. Maybe) I finally took a sensible approach to my job options, I looked at a couple of quality resumes and emulated them. Whether or not I submit them, I feel a lot better about my work history and abilities, just doing this. I scheduled and attended an interview at the Community College and learned about a technical career so far removed from my usual language teaching type career I was inspired and fascinated. I ate a good meal with my family. Then I went to my psychiatrist again.

He pointed out that I will not be instantly better with a new job, in fact my problems could just get buried for awhile. I'm not centered right now, I'm prone to see things from superior or inferior extremes. His overarching advice, advice I will heed: Make No Decisions.

Though I may have put a little more shiny toilet-bowl-esque contact paper on more of the bathroom walls. It is bright and clean looking in there. It makes me laugh when I walk in there.

Day 8: Buy a New Outfit

Friday

Healthy. Eat right. Sober - though for the first time I forgot my friend the sippy cup with straw and sparkly red juice and I wanted a beer. But I prevailed. I bought hot tea. And chicken wraps.

After a work meeting with the union and chief of personnel and my administrator (who now seems to hate me much more than any administrator I have ever worked with) I feel a little relief. My doctor has written a clear note giving me time off and those handy accommodations to keep me away from "hostile and aggressive" people. I think this accommodation might need to be a lifelong requirement for me. The district promised/insisted not to contact me for three weeks. I turned off my work email and my online classroom.

Afterward, I drove with my mom, sister-in-law, and kids to Spokane. I walked by a bunch of friendly looking pubs and bars and imagined the fun of settling in with a beer (or two or ten) and meeting everyone there. But then I thought of being embarrassed and sick and tired. And I thought of myself in ten years, a successful teacher, healthy and fit, my kids healthy and happy....and I drank hot tea. Then I bought a cute, sexy workout outfit. And ate a good dinner. And slept in the car on the way home as my mom and sis-in-law talked and talked.

Then I got home and had amazing sex with my love.

Day 9: Quiet Breakdown at Home Depot

Saturday

I meant to get up and run out and hike with my love. Instead we took our time. I dug out more junk to donate. Wrote.

I'm not sure, but I think it's been nine days now since that night I never slept and cried first thing in the morning until they finally noticed I was suicidal. I told a lot of people, in my own way (like Maria?), but no one heard me until I told the doctor. Thank God.

I am still hurting and vulnerable, prone to melt downs over loud noises and imagined problems. I wept at Home Depot today, overwhelmed by the immensity of available home improvement projects. Entropy. Entropy dragging my home back to mud and wood makes me shut down. It seems we will never have a nice home, it will continue to erode, fall apart. I have no control.

Day 10: Super Bowl Sunday

Sunday

Super Bowl Sunday, when I would normally get drunk and pass out (oops, I mean of course nap) in front of a game I have no interest in. Today I sat quietly, glad to be here and alive and sober and almost free of medication. And I ate a ton of tapenade and clam dip and white chicken chili and even birthday cake for my uncle.

My right foot and ankle were mysteriously bothersome all day. I wrecked it this past summer when, manic and all the other things I do when manic, I stepped in a hole at a party. Two in the morning, it didn't matter, what? Me hurt? Ever since my foot has felt pretty ruined. Not that I stopped me from wearing my Famolare platforms. Or going out dancing. Or getting into bike wrecks.

Anyway, my ankle has been giving me so much trouble the last couple days I've struggled to walk easily. It kept buckling nearly causing me to fall, moving into my knee and hip by Sunday afternoon. I pretended it was fine of course, but then before bed I looked up foot massage. Holly at Chinese Reflexology had some very insightful theories about this type of injury: fear of moving forward. Literally stuck. Wow. Pretty spot on considering my recent intentions and inspirations.

Holly's advice is amazing, I followed her massage guidance plus decided to pay special attention to my kidney spot on my foot - I'm sure my body has some serious toxins it's trying to flush out. I need all the help I can get.

Day 11: Headstand

Monday

Almost pill free. Absolutely over the grip of alcohol/pot/cigarettes/repeat. Totally over my hateful trifecta of self-destruct. Can I safely say never again? Waking up feels good! Since my head no longer hurts I have started beginning each morning with yoga, including a head stand. Starting each day with something so challenging and meditative has been a good way to boost my energy, resolve, and confidence. I'd gotten to the point where I hadn't even tried to do a headstand in….who knows, months, I guess. Whenever this stuff all started spiraling out of control. But now it has become part of my morning routine: wake up, count my blessings, stretch, get out of bed, open my curtains and look at the sky and feel grateful again. I could have died, I might have gone through with it. And why? I was angry at being 'stuck' in a career where I feel helpless? I'm not making the gains I hoped? My best friend hung herself? My students are violent and get stuck in gangs and shoot each other? My colleagues get sick or overwhelmed and complain or quit or kill themselves too? Not worth it! Worth it is the blue sky and the birds returning and the Cypress I planted outside my window. Worth it is knowing my kids are learning to read and are good to be around and loving. Worth it is our vital health. Our safe and comfortable home. Our loving families. Our safety nets that let me take a three week medical emergency to recuperate without worrying (too much) about what will happen to us.

So I begin my new routine, now over a week in and starting to feel like a real routine and not just the substitute it is. I reach my arms up and breathe and do a swan dive, touch my toes, downward facing dog, stretch into cat and cow, enjoy a couple full, healthy, slow sun salutations and end up with my head stand. Where did this headstand even come from? It's like a miracle, this feat of still, suddenly, being able to do a headstand at the age of 39 after giving up on myself so completely. I have the theory that if I tried to do a headstand in the middle of the day I wouldn't be as successful, but since I do it basically before standing up on my feet my body isn't really sure which way I'm supposed to go after laying down all night. I hang there upside down, pointing my toes and feeling proud of myself for the first time in oh so long. Feeling worthwhile. How could I fail today? How could I jump back on that train that was carrying me to my slow death? Not when I can stand on my head!

Leading Up To It

I need to go back and try to remember what happened. How did I get here? I guess it started six months ago…

My journal from last October:

It's almost the Day of the Dead

This week three people died and I'm not doing well. First it was a former colleague, he has mental health issues similar to mine and had been put on administrative leave from work the year before. He got hit by a car, late at night. People are saying it looks like suicide. I was upset by this - could I be put on administrative leave for being erratic too? For crying during our computer training for our state comprehensive evaluation system? Maybe.

Then I started thinking about the next death, a boy in the parking lot of The Pear. At first I didn't think much of it until I read in the newspaper he was shot by two former students, brothers I taught when they were ninth graders. The victim was with another guy who was also shot but who didn't die. He had also been one of my ninth graders, as well as the cousin of my best friend. The shooter and the guy who were shot used to play soccer together. They were sweet 15 year olds. Ugh. My job is stressful.

My meds are whacked. Somehow I got things all mixed up with too many vitamins and no more anti-depressant and I started feeling really weepy and upset. I haven't been able to sleep. Kids at school are not always easy to work with - how could they be? They know these guys too. Some are relatives or neighbors, their parents are worried this could happen to their boys too. Three nights in a row, no sleep, worried and anxious and not eager to return to a job I don't feel I can handle right now.

I woke up Tuesday after just two hours of early morning sleep, tears all over my face. Snot. Pounding head. Frantic and unable to be calm as I lay there silently freaking out in the dark morning. How can I teach fifteen-year-olds like this? How can I teach fifteen-year-olds even if I'm well rested and cheerful when they come from such shit? One girl, her dad murdered her mom then shot himself on the first day of school. Another kid, his mom is in a gang, so are all 6 of his older siblings. Another kid lays his head on his desk all class long, his mom and her white boyfriend kicked him out of the house and his grandma is not taking very good care of him.

I made the right choice and called in sick, sending in some lesson plans I hoped whoever they cobbled together to sub could figure out. I slapped makeup over a falsely cheerful face and got dressed so I could make lunches and breakfast and take good care of my own children, driving them to

48

school, dropping them off on time, telling them I love them, saying nothing about not going to work or dead colleagues or students who shoot each other. I made another good choice and joined my dad and aunt and other older relatives at their regular Tuesday morning retired person breakfast at Clarettes. They were a little surprised to see me, but I cheerfully explained that I had a doctor appointment, as I finished my dad's breakfast. Made polite and happy comments, asked about everyone, smiled and told jokes. Pulled off happy for a little while longer.

Until they asked what time my appointment was and I admitted I didn't have one yet. But I didn't even break down then, it was when they probed further, actually looking at my red-rimmed eyes that makeup couldn't quite hide. Someone asked about school and I melted, mentioning one of my former students shot another of my former students. And my principal wouldn't help me - any of us - wen we needed back up with kids who were struggling. And I can't sleep. Oh...the hugs felt better for a moment, those ol' relatives are nice to me. Thank God for them.

My dad and Aunt Gloria drove me to the doctor. Gloria prayed with me. The doctor talked to me and got me on medicine that is supposed to help me even out and sleep. My dad and I went on a long bike ride. I would be OK. I could handle this. Except when we got home from the bike ride there was a text message saying my best friend Maria was dead. I somehow knew what it was going to say even before I read the whole thing. Deep in the darkness in my mind I guess I knew she was suicidal, though even now I have nothing I can put my finger on for how I knew. And of course, if I knew - why, why, why didn't I do anything for her? I stared at that text and felt like I was in a dream.

My first thought was, Why didn't Maria tell me? But of course, why would Maria tell me she was dead? And who else would think to tell me since she is in the middle of a bitter divorce and her mom lives in another country and her daughters are in elementary school (noooooooooo!!!!!!!!!) and she has no brothers or sisters. In fact, I still don't even know who sent this text, maybe a cousin just went through her phone and texted people? I don't know. I guess I'll figure it out at her funeral..

Oh, did I mention how she died? She hung herself. My best friend hung herself. I can't even write anymore. I don't have anything to quip about that. Just, it's almost the Day of the Dead and death is swirling around. Again.

I Can Freak Out Tomorrow

13 Days Ago
The Day Before Day 1

The last Thursday in January

I wonder if I ate, in one swoop, all that
medicine they've given me over the years if I'd
die. Would I? Or would I just fuck myself up and
then be even worse off - on some machine or
unable to ever drink again or just really sick? Or if
I crashed into a big semi on the highway like I
almost did last Friday night, would I actually die?

Or just be a useless quadriplegic, head on a pillow, unable to kill myself or make it better.

Not to mention my kids, my love. My parents, my brothers. A few of my cousins and aunts and uncles - well some - would be upset. Some wold love it. They could gloat over it for days, imagine my bitchy cousin Kareen? She'd love it, I'd finally be out of her hair. But a lot of people would not like it. Like how I felt, with Maria, or Jon or Scott or even people I hardly know like Tami and my love's uncle. Suicide is brutal. It's mean. But I still see it as the most logical solution at times. Then I think, if faced with the idea of death then I see the idea of different schedules I won kj;sea's fj ;al. ;Ajsitopei jai;j fja;

Day 12

Day 12

I am off almost everything now: Fluoxetine, Topiramate, Citalopram, alcohol, cigarettes, marijuana. The chemistry set is nearly empty, only the nightly sleeping pill remains - and I'll have to get off that too. Last night I "forgot" it, hoping I could just be clean-brained, healed! Yay, all better! But…I had trouble sleeping? Coincidence? Or over-stimulation at my first big (read: loud) social event since Freak Out, Day 1.

Twelve days ago I checked out of my life.
Boom. Done. And I didn't have to kill myself to
do it. When I woke up that next morning I was
already crying. I looked at my journal, saw the
crazy ideas I had written while half-asleep, and
told my love: I need help. He asked if I wanted
him to take me to the doctor, and I laughed, said I
happened to have an appointment in an hour for
my annual pap smear. Then I cried when I
imagined that cold silver thing shoved inside of
me.

But the doctor did help me, like a miracle she
heard me when I told her I wasn't doing well. And
now I'm doing better. But damn, I made a big
public scene when I left the school, didn't I? I
walked out of a class that I had lost control of (OK,
maybe walking out isn't exactly true, I just
dismissed them two minutes early and then was the
first one out the door). But I FELT like walking
out. And I really did walk out in my own head.

Then I went down to the office to ask for help;
and I ended up losing my shit in front of all the
secretaries and the principal when I was offered
scorn, not support. (Ok, maybe losing my shit is

an exaggeration too. I started crying and scowled for a moment…but I felt like I was losing my shit). I will not return to that place ever again. I will never teach again. I am free.

Or OK, who knows? The psychiatrist said it is really important I make no decisions right now. But…I do feel free. My path to a positive, meaningful, fulfilling life is falling into place. My steps:
   - Be healthy and clear headed
   - Sleep at night
   - Ask for help
   - Pay attention to my dreams
   - Be thankful
   - Clear negative clutter from my life
   - Keep my real goals clear
   - Pray
   - Listen
   - Be positive and hopeful for a good life

Time for a new life. A life with my family where they can be proud of my ability to be strong, healthy and able to make positive changes. I need to choose a better life, work for it, be successful and content with it.

Day 13: Let the Waves Wash it Away

Day 13

The kids and I were lucky enough to be able to travel to the Oregon Coast. My friend Theresa invited us. Just getting out of town cleared my mind of residual stress. I completely forgot my own mind and fears, especially when her sweet elderly dog, Bella, had an accident in the back of the car. Helping someone in need is therapeutic, even if all four of us were gagging as we cleaned. Oh man that cup holder though….

I did make the mistake of reading an old People magazine once we got to the beach house. What poison! It's 3 am and I just woke up after a hideous nightmare directly related to the garbage I read: little girl abductions, adultery, more abductions with icky horrible motives and women held in captivity for years as slaves. Then photographs, heavily photoshopped, of women in bikinis. She lost 250 pounds! She just had a baby! She rocks her killer bod! As if the literal shape of a woman's body gives her worth. I guess it does...to sexual predators who kidnap women and girls for sex. Thanks People Magazine. Never, never again. Never.

Moving on, I can't get mired down in that. Since I'm awake (not my bed, strange sounds, ate chips at 10 pm plus tons of afternoon caffeine to drive) I will move in a positive direction: the Depak Chopra and Oprah meditation! Yes, good vibes. (I make better choices every day)

Day 14: Survival Instinct

Day 14

For over a year I've been saying I want to spend February in the sunshine at the coast. It was one of those power of positive thinking things, you know….write it down, it will happen. Believe it and you will see it. All these nice ideas that I really want to be true but I sometimes despair at because some things never seem to come to fruition.

The last time I travelled to the coast it was with Dex - no! Don't think about Dex! Distraction. Think about anything else.

However, here it is, February, and I am sitting here on the second story balcony of my friend, Theresa's house. The Pacific Ocean is...I don't know, math hurts my brain still....but like a 30 second walk from where I stand. Just a small green patch of grass, a bank of rocks, and the waves at high tide rolling in. The sun is shining. SHINING so bright I am warm and cozy sitting outside. Did I mention it is February? My kids and I started the day off on the beach, I was a little confused about what the ocean is like, so I brought a big bag of blankets and books and my computer thinking I'd just sit there. But Winston wouldn't just sit, he's 8. Cody and Sam sat for a moment longer, but they wanted to race the waves too. So I ended up tossing my bag to safety and running, terrorized, into the water after them when they got too close to a large wave and were suddenly all hip deep in water. Sam and Winston bolted to safety, but Cody started to fall. I was gripped with a maniacal horror as the water welled around us. Stories of drownings and tsunamis and People magazine sensationalism washed over me worse than the waves lapping around my knees. Grabbing his hand I hauled him up and toward the safety of the dry sand. He picked up on my fear and raced ahead, but my pesky ankle gave out, twisted, and buckled under me. I nearly fell. The wave was now subsiding as I continued hobbling up the shore, looking over my shoulder to make sure no more water was coming up to drown me. Wow, for someone hell-bent on suicide two weeks ago I suddenly gathered some kind of survival instinct, huh?

The strangest thing, though, was that by the time I reached my dry log my ankle had straightened out and no longer hurt. I gave a couple of tentative steps, putting a little pressure on it...and it didn't fold in or buckle or even twinge. Was Holly at the Chinese Reflexology website right? Was my fear just settling into my legs and ankles? Am I really just frozen in fear?

Day 15: Frozen

Day 15

First day without any medication, now weened off the anti-depressants, the anti-anxiety pills. Not to mention no alcohol or pot or cigarettes. Wow, you know what that means? For the first in in…I don't know, many years, four years, I am just me. Sure it's only been two weeks or twelve days, but I am free.

Recuperating at the beach. Lots of tasty food, kid movies, walks on the beach. I started writing, working, enjoying the sunshine as I looked out over the ocean. Then the internet blitzed out - oddly enough just as I typed the word "Froze". I suddenly could not use my phone or computer (no email, social media, writing program, or internet).

Providence, I suppose. After getting over my initial anxiety, I relaxed and focused on the present. Read, played tag with the kids, played dominoes, scrabble, memory. Went in the hot tub. Cleaned up. In the afternoon I joined Theresa and the kids on an excursion to the dollar store. I got a good laugh (my first this year) at Cody and Sam and a bunch of new acquaintances (one of whom was also named Sam) in the toy aisle running around with fairy wings and nerf swords. It was a good day for relaxing and healing.

Yes, I struggled briefly while we were driving around Lincoln City and - depressed, overly-sprawled town that it is - I looked out the car window and saw bar after bar. Beer! Liquor! Karaoke! I had forgotten to bring my sparkling water, juice, or even plain water and I was momentarily agitated. Maybe low blood-sugar. We went to one cheap, overcrowded store after the next and I couldn't find one can or bottle of Peregrino or even plain water or natural juice. Just crappy high-fructose corn syrup pop and juice-type drinks. Oh, and tons and tons of beer, wine, mixers, liquor, cigarettes and wine coolers. I had to get out of those stores! It was dinner time, my body was feeling whacked, and I couldn't find relief.

It's funny how I get as grumpy about shitty high-fructose corn syrup/sugar drinks as I do about alcohol, but there you have it. I am not going through all of this just to get addicted to Pepsi or Froot Punch. Or this is what my addled and fragile brain reasoned. Really, I just had a bad moment.

But a health food store miraculously appeared. I screamed at Theresa to stop the car, I jumped out and bought sparkling water, ginger ale, pomegranate juice, and maca tea. I guzzled the sweet tea...and cravings were gone. Hello substitutions!

Day 16

Day 16

Blessedly uneventful. We drove home.

Yesterday was a good day, pretty much. But a couple of times I started to lose it. I caught myself, but I scared the kids for a second. There was the TV - too loud, blaring ads. I had a pot boiling with water, trying to dislodge caked-on cheese that wouldn't come out, crap cheese stuck everywhere - sponge, sink, definitely the pot. Then Cody yelled, over, the din of the commercials, that he had broken my awesome new steam punk goggles again. Ugh! Boiling water! Loud TV! Meticulous re-buckling of goggles over top hat (now covered with dog hair!)

For about three minutes I just spewed words, vitriolic torrent of words. My new goggles are cheap, what a waste! That stupid TV, gah!! It's bedtime!!

The kids grew silent. I fixed the goggle buckle. The TV was silenced. I get tired of vacation and I want to go home. I need my routine. I haven't been alone - not to even sleep or go to the bathroom - all week. Off my calming drugs, nothing to soothe my agitated mind.

I got calm. I had eaten too much sugar, eaten dinner too late. Our stuff was strewn about. But then we put on 'My Big Fat Greek Wedding' (without commercials), turned the lights down, fireplace on. Dishes done. Kids happy, forgiveness and love.

Day 17

Back Home

My love and I argued briefly tonight because he didn't want to leave a loud party and I felt overwhelmed. I wonder if I will be ale to maintain any of my current relationships? I don't have that many real friends anyway, do I? Just people I get (GOT) drunk with, right?

Before it gets better I guess it could still keep being bad, right? Or is only crying twice today OK? People from work must have received my shameful sick leave request today. A few people reached out, probably in kindness, but…all I could do was cry. So I fumbled through responses. I need to figure out what to say. I can't go around telling people I wanted to kill myself. Or I couldn't stop crying. Or I was on a ton of medication and other crap and everything just came tumbling down. Right? What do you tell people?

I have been paying attention to my dreams, like the psychiatrist said I should. Not going to bed drunk seems to be helping me sleep and my dreams are vivid. But they seem to be dredging up old stuff. Really old stuff. I've dreamed of Will a couple of times (hiding, writing him a letter) but the dreams about Dex are really bothersome. Dex? It's been years, really, like four or five - I can't think of how many, numbers still hurt my head. But many, many years. I didn't think he even mattered, but there are the dreams. Him walking away. Driving a car. In the distance.

Is this one of those things I'm going to have to work through? I expected Maria, of course. Four months ago my best friend told me how unhappy she was and I just told her, like it's no big deal, that she'll feel better (like ME!) in a few years. No worry. Let's hang out this weekend, we'll have fun!!!!

Then she goes and hangs herself a couple of days later. I'm really not sure how I'll deal with that one. Thinking of hanging myself a few months later might have been one way. I've always been very empathetic.

But back to Dex, maybe I need to give that a little thought. He was such a big part of my life for so long, it was so terrible when it ended….that's when I started drinking and smoking all the time, not just occasionally. That seemed to be the tipping point for me.

What happened?

Dex: Finally Dealing with that Asshole

Four(ish) Years Ago

Saturday night should be fun. Really, really fun. People should crowd my home, eating, drinking, playing cards, dancing, singing along to some talented musicians playing in the corner. So what if last night I went out with my friend Sonara (and somehow became the third wheel when her new boyfriend joined us) and ended up on stage at The 100 singing 'Satin Doll' with a professional jazz band? See - sometimes being bad does pay. That was a magical break from the norm and has only served to make me more unhappy with my current lame situation. More on that later. But Saturday night should be phenomenal! Blazing with good times, a million eligible bachelors all in love with me!

Oh wait. That's not reality, that's some movie or a chick lit novel. Sounds right up my alley, though. I usually try to figure out a way for some version of this every Friday and Saturday night - though I suspect not everyone else in this world feels life should be so exciting and stimulating or even require this much effort. My mom thinks I need to be content alone, do some art project or watch TV and be OK with no social life. Like her.

Most of the other young moms I know are happy with this kind of existence - though they all have husbands to keep them company, not psycho ex-husbands who threaten to kill them. Well, who knows - domestic violence is pretty easy to hide, I have some suspicions about some of the couples I know. I have an eye for it now. I know about that bratty ninth grader in my second period. I've met *her asshole dad, I know he's abusive somehow. I know her mom is afraid of him and he loves it. Just like his kid tries to make all the kids at school afraid of her.*

Sure, most moms don't have freaky ex-husbands, I am aware of this. I know most men are just going about their boring man business, being good husbands and helping their wives to live good upstanding lives. And all those friends that used to invite us to their parties, who we joined for vacations, who called for play dates? They don't contact me much anymore. Something about icky tragedy in middle class circles causes dignified people to become scarce. It's like when you smash an ant and all the other ants instantly start swarming for awhile but then eventually they leave it alone to writhe around in it's agony alone. Did you ever wonder what those ants were doing? I'll tell you - the same thing all my friends and neighbors and colleagues were doing three years ago when my life fell apart: they're asking that ant to describe the horror. Those swarming ants are wide-eyed, devouring the tragedy, asking the smashed ant - it's little abdomen all crumpled, missing a couple legs - "What happened? Didn't you suspect it would get this bad? Why didn't you leave? Or fight back? I would have." Then they swarm away to their happy lives, relieved that this time tragedy didn't strike their home. The offering was made to the gods and they are safe for now.

So, yeah, I've spent a few evenings alone since then. I try to go out, I do get invited, but not much. My mom says the tragedy of my past coupled with the way I look makes married ladies not too eager to have me be the lone single woman at their table - they don't want their husbands to fall in love. That's nice of her to say...though I suspect it's not true. I think I'm just not a huge asset to social circles anymore. You know, "Rich, Marsha, I'd like you to meet Amanda, the cute little beaten ex-wife of the guy you bowled with?" Somehow that just doesn't fly at dinner parties. So in the past three years I've been a good mom to my poor little fatherless boys, moved into a pretty house, taught school and aerobics classes. I've gone out with some old friends who are too wild but fun, made friends from church, tried to have a boyfriend (ouch!), got certified to teach yoga...and about a thousand other things (good and bad) to try to fill my time. Is it better? Sure, much better. But I'm still home alone on a Saturday night - hey! My friend Maria just texted, she and Penny are coming over to play a board game. Allll riiiight!

Am I manic? My doctor diagnosed me as bipolar last summer - just a few months before I started dating his younger brother. Damn it, I haven't seen that guy in two weeks and he still has my favorite underwear - the turquoise and mint green g-string. I wonder what he did with them after I told him I loved him but then that I can't see him any more because we're both too screwed up to date? Are they on top of his dryer? Or in his bedside table drawer, next to the gun and condoms? Or on the kitchen table with the unpaid bills?

I think I really like that guy. Really a lot. He's multi-talented, decent - like a healthy dessert. Even though he may be right about us being wrong for each other. Or maybe not, he isn't sure. Or maybe this is love or we are right or with time he'll be ready or maybe we would be happy if we got married or maybe he didn't date around enough? Pretty frustrating, but amazingly understandable. I

*wonder where he is tonight? Has he forgotten me,
moved on?*

*And uhhhhh....am I manic? What the hell?
Just because I stay up all night for no reason does
that make me manic? I promise I rarely do
anything really crazy or out of control. I really
don't even get that drunk. And I never do any of it
if I have to be responsible. My kids are well-cared
for and my family thinks I'm great. It's just that
every two weeks and every other Tuesday night
their dad takes my babies away from me. And I
would die if I didn't have some escape. What
woman wouldn't? So every two weeks he comes
and takes my little guys for a visit (which they
love) and I call Maria or Penny or Geri or Sonara.*

*You can judge if you want. But keep in mind
that every night, Monday through Friday plus
every other weekend, I have my three boys fed and
bathed and in bed by 8 pm, I read to them, I sing to
them, and I pray with them. This is after a good
home-cooked meal and teaching high school.
Perfect. Perfect. Perfect. And then I fall apart.
Bad, really. But only for a moment while I can or
have to or whatever. So you can sit there and look*

down on me. But I challenge you to do any better if what happened to me happened to you. If you had to endure what I went through with an infant and two toddlers, let's see what you do. Would you just quietly put up with it? When your kids went away, would you be all excited like Yeah!!! I can watch whatever I want on TV! Again. Since my kids are in bed every night at 8:00 I could always watch whatever I want on TV. And since I detest TV and don't have internet or cable and don't spend my time watching TV I guess this whole argument is idiotic.

Because the the thing is, some people like to watch life happen and some people like to make life happen. Or at least sit in a drunken stupor and throw in the occasional sentence reflecting on life that is happening in reality around them. That's me. I live. If you want to sit on your ass and watch people in Los Angeles show you some plasticized version of how life might look, go ahead. For me, I will go out and watch it first hand. Plus jump up on stage or onto a barstool or just into the middle of a conversation and live. Way more entertaining than HBO.

Maria and Penny came over tonight after my babies went to sleep. We played Scattergories and laughed and had fun. Wow. I realize these girls get me. I can be honest and express my beliefs and talk about my interests and ideas and preferences and I'm not weird. Same world. Same point of references. No judgement or crassness or superiority. No scrappy jealousy or competition or flat out disregard for my likes, like Dex and his friends.

Dexterous is wrong for me. Just because I like how he looks physically, he makes me laugh, he's everything a man "should" be....doesn't mean we're a good fit. That uneducated bimbo hairdresser his friends brought along on the camping trip I wasn't supposed to be at - she is a good match for him. Lower class, nasty, cheap food, reality TV on a BIG SCREEN, no books! Loud expensive toys, hunting, store-bought cookies, easy, sweet liquor drinks, horses. Yes, this is D's world. Cheap. Crass. Dime a dozen. Easy.

Me? I'm none of this, which I guess makes me difficult. I'm not a good match for his world. I'm too educated, too well read and free-thinking. Too *pretty, too athletic, too classy. Too dignified, too structured, too disciplined.*

My world is taking walks through town while conversing with loved ones, ethnic food, camping with inner tubes or hiking with cards and ghost stories by the camp fire. Cooking, games, music and conversation at home with loved ones. Listening to books read aloud. Bike rides. Reading the newspaper and drinking coffee on the front porch. Working together to make a beautiful home. Time with kids - activities geared toward them: parks, community events, parties where kids are invited, family meals.

How sad, in nine months of dating, Dexterous and I never did most of my favorite things. He never once joined my kids and me for a meal at home and with my family maybe four times. Though his friends have kids the exact age as my mine, we never got together as a group with the kids. They only socialize all girls (and never invited me. I get the hint) or all guys (at the bar, led by Married-But-Looking). We took one walk - the night we met (oh! why did that have to be so magical?). None of his friends ride bikes or read or care about education. Camping? No one tells stories or plays games or hikes or does anything athletic - they just drink a LOT, drive a boat, and fish - which was fun, but still...

Newspaper? Coffee? Nope - TV and Diet Pepsi. Games? He doesn't like them. Even our taste in movies and music doesn't match. He likes low-brow, stupid, immature potty joke movies or mindless action-flix. I like complex plots and character development.

Spiritually - he is dogmatic, will not venture out of his comfort zone to even listen to an idea different from his. Any other religion is just wrong. Politics too - Democrats are just stupid and emotional.

Blow him off.

When I think of my part or of Dex, I know I am better off now. I have lived in the same small town nearly all of my life, and I know my life looks pretty good from the outside, though inside I am slowly dying. Divorced, the mother of three young boys, I have taught high school Spanish for 7 years. Without child support, I can barely make ends meet. I need to stand up for myself, to come out of my shell, to be a free woman. But this hadn't started out very well.

Watching my house and car fall apart while working long hours at a thankless job, I despair while I try to figure out what to do with my life, how I will be able to support these boys. I hate being a burden on my big brother, Charlie, though I often trade meals for minor home repairs. I have tried to date since my life fell apart, but after Dex I attempted to date a man was way too young for me and turned out to be too needy. And Dex wasn't worth my time. He was a successful engineer, but after declaring me and my boys "not the whole package" one night, I realized he was never going to marry me so I broke up with him. Now I am single and have been for over a year, I date occasionally. I am even considering trying the internet, but no one has clicked.

I keep wondering about Dex. What happened? Even though I knew it was going no where and broke up with him I still kept seeing him. Well - I admit it, even now I still see him sometimes. I just can't seem to end it.

Dexterous was so sweet and attentive when we first met. I was thrilled! After all my struggle to trust again, after the loss and pain, I had finally met someone worth dating. I was over the moon. After just a few dates I felt a swirling of love all around me. I didn't want to admit it, but I was convinced we would be married by the end of the year.

Dex and I met at a dinner party, at my friend Sonara's house last winter. She has worked in his office building for a few years and she had mentioned him to me. She was so excited about him that at first I thought maybe she liked him for herself, but she and Chris had been dating for a few months and she was really into him. So when I saw him at her house during her Christmas party,

I was already prepared to like him. And he didn't disappoint me. It turned out his older brother was my doctor. I had't even put the two of them together, but of course they are brothers. It was kind of weird when we first started dating, I hoped Dr. D wouldn't reveal any of my secrets. Especially that manic idea, I know people are supposed to be OK with mental health issues now days, but being bi-polar (really - I'm still not convinced I even am) is such a messed up thing to be.

But Dex seemed to really like me. In fact, he got my phone number while we were at Sonara's and the very next night he called. He didn't even seem to mind my little boy chaos going around me as I tried talking to him.

Our First Date, about four years ago:

Our first date! It was only a few days after we met, my last night of my Christmas break. Dex had come to pick me up, surprising my when he showed up in a huge diesel truck complete with gun rack. I have to admit, even though I'm more of an electric car kind of girl I felt really safe and protected by his big manly man truck.

We went to one of my favorite restaurants, Brasserie, and he was so attentive and gentlemanly. He even pulled my chair out for me.

"How do you like being a teacher?" He asked.

I smiled, I couldn't stop smiling! "Well, I like the kids, but the meetings and paperwork are getting worse every year. But it's still a fun job. How about you? How is the world of engineering?."

He had smiled, his sweet brown eyes crinkling as he talked about how much he enjoyed machines and lasers. I laughed to myself at his enthusiasm, it was not my area of interest - at all! - But he was cute as he talked about catalytic converters and laser food analysis machines.

I tried to pay attention, too, but his lips were so soft-looking I just wanted to kiss him! I managed to constrain myself throughout the meal, but once we were done eating he invited me to walk with him. We walked slowly around downtown, talking about nothing and everything.

"My wife left me a couple of years ago," he told me sadly. "She wanted to move to the city and get her Masters in business administration. I didn't want to move and she did. It was like she was just looking for an excuse, she hardly discussed it with me at all. One day she just informed me she was going to Seattle, she was starting school in a few weeks and she had an apartment."

"That's sad," I said, trying to ignore the fact that he'd called her his wife, not his ex-wife, "didn't you try to follow her?"

He looked pained, "No, maybe I should have. Her parents were mad at me that I didn't. Her dad said I should fight for her. But if she didn't want to work it out with me, how could I make her love me again?"

My heart hurt for him. I wished I could fix it for him.

He looked sweetly down at me, I felt so secure and cared for next to his big frame. He smiled, "You know, my house is just so sad now. It needs light and life. I want to turn it into a home again."

My heart leapt. A home! I felt a surge of hope, maybe this was the guy. THE GUY. After nearly two years of being the pathetic abandoned divorcee maybe I had finally discovered my match, the guy who would be my best friend and who would take care of me and my kids. The man who was honorable and upstanding. Everything Will was not.

I smiled back and said, "I would love to see your place."

And then, best of all, we walked to the park so we could see the gazebo in the moonlight. That's where he finally turned to me and took me in his arms, holding me and humming as we danced around the gazebo, kissing me in the moonlight. Sigh.

He pulled back, looking deep into my eyes. "Are you dating anyone?" he asked, suddenly urgent. I shook my head. The relief on his face before he kissed me again sent a flutter through my chest.

The very next afternoon he looked me up, sent me an email (so what if he spelled my name wrong!). Now this is one guy I don't mind looking me up, so much better than those two weirdos last year.

From: dexterousdoesit@engineeringfirm.com
To: TeacherAmanda@hometownmail.com
Subject: Movie?
January 4 at 8:05 AM

Hi Amannda,

How are you? How are all your students? I bet they are rowdy today being the first day back. I know I am a little rambunctious; hard to stay in my seat.

Do you want to watch a movie? I mentioned you to my brother and sister-in-law and they rented the newest 'Ice Brigade' movie. They thought we might want to watch it. I could bring it in this evening after I do some chores?

What days are you available for lunch? Do you have an hour or 1/2 hour?

Just wanted to let you know I have been thinking about you.

Dexterous

From: TeacherAmanda@hometownmail.com
To: dexterousdoesit@engineeringfirm.com
RE: Movie?
January 4 at 8:45 AM

Hey Deex great to hear from you.

I've been thinking about you ;)

Yes, I'd love to see you (and watch the movie too, of course!) After 8 would be perfect.

I'll talk to you soon!
Amanda

From: TeacherAmanda@hometownmail.com
To: dexterousdoesit@engineeringfirm.com
Subject: Good Morning!
January 5 at 8:47 AM

Hi Deexterous :)
I hope you woke up well, I know I did....I feel so great I think somehow I managed to squeeze a full night's rest into 3 hours. Hmmmm wonder why...
Have a great day
Amanda

From: dexterousdoesit@engineeringfirm.com
To: TeacherAmanda@hometownmail.com
RE: Good Morning!
January 7 at 2:10 PM (That's two days later!)

Hi Amanda
Sorry I was spelling your name wrong. I'm a little dyslexic.

I felt a little slow this morning. I had a drainage problem at the house. had a bit of an ice dam and the water was not able to flow away from the foundation. Got her fixed. Nothing serious.

I feel pretty good right now. The 2:00 pm hour is my weak hour.

I was going to send this last night, I got busy

Have a great day

Deexterous

From: TeacherAmanda@hometownmail.com
To: dexterousdoesit@engineeringfirm.com
Subject: Good to hear from you!
January 7 at 8:10 PM

Hey Dexterous

How are feeling today? More rested than yesterday, I hope! Let's not stay up that late again on a work night...but it was sure nice getting to know you even better. I start getting silly and hyper the less sleep I get - not to mention slow to come up with words and overly honest. School yesterday was great, so nice to see my kids again after almost three weeks, but I was so groggy they were starting to take advantage of me - they talked me into extra time in the computer lab.

You asked me the other night about lunch. For the next two weeks I only have 30 minutes, not nearly enough time to go anywhere. But maybe you would like to join us for dinner some night? I love making things in the crock pot, so even a work night would be fine.

Have a great rest of your day Dex.
Amanda

From: dexterousdoesit@engineeringfirm.com
To: TeacherAmanda@hometownmail.com
RE: Good to hear from you
January 8 at 9:00 PM (I didn't see this one until the next day)

Hi Amanda,

Thanks for the note. I am having a busy day. Things are starting to Roll again. Many deadlines between now and the end of the month.

I slept well last night. Still not on my work schedule for sleep. I hope you have a good time with you family this evening. I might hang out with Mike for a while this evening?

Don't bother with the crock pot. We can go out for dinner, and yes, no staying up so late.
Dex

From: dexterousdoesit@engineeringfirm.com
To: TeacherAmanda@hometownmail.com
RE: Good to hear from you
January 9 at 2:14 PM

Hmmm, I wrote this yesterday and thought I sent it. That is how my days go. I can get bombarded with things. Another issue needing resolution comes prior to finishing the last.

I am sorry I did not get this sent. As discussed the other day I will see you shortly after 8:00.

I hope you are having a great day.

Talk to you soon

Dex

Do you notice how the emails went from frequent, romantic, and promising to….occasional and logistical? Maybe you didn't because you have always been a relaxed person with a fairly smoothly running life. I, on the other hand, was a single mother of three tiny boys trying to figure out for the first time after ten years in a scary marriage. I tried to be calm, I really did. I called my girlfriends and got them to help me not get too over my head. But after so long being single, nervous of all men, scared Will would follow through with his threats that he would kill me eventually, I couldn't just relax. I was thrilled to have met Dex. But - somehow I wasn't feeling very good, I was just too anxious. I nearly had a panic attack after our second date when I sent him a friendly email and he totally ignored me for two days. Sure, he responded eventually with how busy he was and even the email he thought he had sent, but I had still spent the night before wondering what had happened. And it wasn't like he was calling or texting. Email seemed to be his favorite form of communication, and he wasn't very consistent. What was up with delay on the email? I'm sure being an engineer is super stressful and all, but so is being a teacher and I can manage to shoot off a quick response to emails. If they are important. And I was starting to wonder, just two weeks into this tentative relationship, if I was even important to him. His actions were inconsistent and I was feeling very anxious.

Not to mention, I had put myself out there and invited him to come for dinner and he didn't even acknowledge my invitation. What is that?

No surprise, really, because he had come to my house with the movie from his brother (isn't that awesome! He even told his family about me!!). The boys were all asleep and Dex and I did not watch even five minutes of that movie. Instead we talked and…kissed. And kissed some more. And kissed some more. I was so into that guy.

But you see? Not hearing from him after making out on my couch for basically six hours? I figured he just thought I was a slutty, cheap, easy woman and not worth his high standards. I was pretty devastated. Then he wrote back and I was thrilled. From the moment I met him it was like a roller coaster, and I don't think it was really his fault, just that somehow what I needed and what he could give just didn't…quite…click. I figured maybe email wasn't the best way to talk to him, some people just don't have the same ideas about email, right? He was like that with texts, though too. Maybe even worse. God, I can't stand it when people don't respond to emails or text messages. Just respond, damn it! Just reply with the letter K or a smiley face or something, ignoring someone's text is so rude.

I would get all anxious almost every time we communicated. Normally, if someone sends me a text or an email or calls me I get it right away. I'm high-strung that way, I hate having a bunch of people to respond to so I always respond as soon as I can. I never leave unanswered stuff just lying around, it makes me really anxious. But with Dex, he was so slow to respond that I would purposefully hold off on responding to him too. Who wants to be that desperate lady who sends an email then gets a response two days later and then immediately responds? Reeks of total desperation, not to mention not having a life. Which admittedly, I didn't really have much of a life beyond teaching people how to conjugate verbs and caring for small boys.

But once we were together I forgot all about my anxiety, mainly because I was so head over heels for him nothing else mattered. I loved his deep voice and kind eyes and being in his big strong arms. He was funny and sweet and could fix anything. And when we kissed - ! I was embarrassed at how much I cared for him. I didn't have sex until we had been dating three weeks, even though I had I had to exercise all my constraint. I really wanted to earlier. But I didn't because I wanted to wait until…I don't know, marriage? I just wanted to be sure it was real. The worst thing was, though, as soon as I finally had sex with him he pulled back even more. After that he only called or emailed every four or five days. I was a mess. What had happened? What had happened to the romantic promise of our first date?

But I kept seeing him, trying to make it work, almost getting to a point of being stable and happy. Somehow, though, he just never felt right. He was sweet and considerate, we had some fun together, but he just didn't get me. I tried to pretend he did…but he didn't.

From: dexterousdoesit@engineeringfirm.com
To: TeacherAmanda@hometownmail.com
Subject: Hi
January 20 at 9:00 AM

Hi,

I know you are not at work today. Thought It would be nice to start your day with a hello, so...... Hello!

I had a strange day/night last night.

I never napped yesterday. Lounged and watched some "boy" movies... SCI FI stuff. Went to bed around 10 slept well until 5:00 am then could not sleep very well of course until just before the alarm. Usually the early morning is when I sleep the best. Curious.

Anyway have a great day

Dex

From: TeacherAmanda@hometownmail.com
To: dexterousdoesit@engineeringfirm.com
RE: Hi
January 21 at 1:00 PM

Hi to you too Dexterous!

Sorry to hear you didn't sleep well last night...I hope you have a better night tonight. I always sleep better if I exercise and I'm going to teach my yoga class in about 15 minutes. Yay! I love teaching yoga, besides getting some really great exercise I also get to see people feeling proud of themselves for working hard at something.

Work was so great today, we are finally back into a regular routine, it always takes awhile after Christmas Break. I think I'll be going out to eat tomorrow from 11:30 to 12:10 if you're interested in meeting me someplace quick. I'm not sure if that's your lunch time or if you're busy with your guys from Mexico. I'm pretty sure I'll be on my hour lunch schedule next week 11:30 to 12:30, so keep that in mind too.

I have my book club tonight, so glad. I love seeing those girls. I couldn't read the book though - too violent and scary, it was about Vietnam and I just can't handle those kind any more. Our joke is that no one ever reads the book, we're just there for the wine and conversation!

Would you like to have lunch tomorrow?

I hope you have a good night. See you soon.
Amanda

From: dexterousdoesit@engineeringfirm.com
To: TeacherAmanda@hometownmail.com
RE: Hi
January 22 at 5:00 PM

Well, Just leaving work.

I know I could use some exercise. It always helps. Maybe next week right?

I am going to take the guys to a fast food dinner and head home.

I hope you have a good morning and I hope you had fun at your book club.

Talk to you soon

Dex

See what I mean about the emails? I asked him if he wanted to go to lunch and he didn't even bother to respond that same day, much less to acknowledge my invitation. Doesn't he know I was totally putting myself out there, inviting him to have lunch? It's really embarrassing to ask a guy to hang out, it looks pretty pushy and needy and all sorts of other tacky and I was nervous about even asking. Now, after three weeks of dating I had invited him once to dinner and once to eat lunch, and he just brushed off both of my invitations. Ouch.

The ladies in book club were my saving grace. We would get together once a month, drink some wine, share about our lives…Oh! And talk about books a little bit too.

My drama with Dexterous was pretty interesting for everyone. I think because I was so pitiful for so long, this poor little abused thing with three very small children, they were just hoping I'd find love. But ugh! I felt this swirling panic whenever I thought of love or marriage or a relationship. Dex just wasn't stepping up like I thought he would on that first amazing night. I kept hoping he'd be that guy again, but he skirted around the idea of us.

What happened to the guy who wanted a home and a family? What happened to the guy who looked at me with love and wanted to be certain I'm not dating anyone else? Where did the guy go who is so excited about me he send me an email the very next day, inviting me out for dinner?

Suddenly he was cold - not mean or unfriendly - just not...in love. Three weeks in, and now his stupid emails were about work and exercise and what he had for dinner. I invited him for lunch and he didn't even acknowledge it, just said nah, going with the guys. What the hell is that? And of course my friends notice the change. They were so thrilled that poor little Amanda finally found someone to protect her and her children from the psycho ex-husband, finally could be alone with a man again, finally was excited about the possibility of love.

Then pathetic Amanda is evasive and doesn't really want to talk about him and asks if it's weird if he turns down dinner invitations or doesn't make any kind of weekend plans until Friday night. When it's too late and she has no babysitter. So they suspected, right away, that things weren't quite right.

From: TeacherAmanda@hometownmail.com
To: Sonar@gogetthatmail.com, PennyP@hometownmail.com, Maria@gogetthatmailcom, Geri@bankloancentral.com, EmilynGreg@hometownmail.com
Subject: Next Book Club
January 21, 9:30 PM

Hello Book Club Ladies!
Thanks for the fun night girls! Our next book club meeting is Tuesday February 10 at 7 pm at

Geri's house. We will read 'Me Talk Pretty One Day' by David Sedaris.

See you then!
Amanda

From: maria@gogetthatmail.com
To: TeacherAmanda@hometownmail.com
RE: Next Book Club
January 24 at 10:30 AM

Hey pretty lady!

So so so good to see you last night, I can't believe you are dating Dex! He's a catch and perfect for you. I want to hear all about it.

Do you want to go with a group of us to Main Street? There's supposed to be a fun band playing.

Mar

From: TeacherAmanda@hometownmail.com
To: maria@gogetthatmail.com
RE: Next Book Club
January 24 at 11:05 AM

Hi Maria

Yeah the whole dating thing is so scary for me...I feel a little anxious even though he has been so great and makes me feel like he cares. I guess I'm just used to the comfort of being either married or single, this half way thing is really strange. But maybe it could be considered fun, huh?

Yes, I'd love to go with you guys tonight. Will has the boys so I'm free. I kind of thought Dex would ask me out? Aren't guys supposed to do that? Ugh, I wish this was more fun. Oh well, you guys will all be so much more chill, thanks again! See you tonight.

Amanda

From: maria@gogetthatmail.com
To: TeacherAmanda@hometownmail.com
RE: Next Book Club
January 24 at 11:15 AM

I always enjoyed dating. Kind of miss it. If you're not comfortable in a relationship--life's too short to suffer through it. Either make yourself comfortable, or get out. :-)

Seems like you guys are doing great, though, so I wouldn't worry about it. If you're not comfortable having sex without knowing for sure he's your boyfriend, and is not sleeping with anyone else, then you could always wait. (Even if you already have.)

You're an awesome woman. He's probably just scared because he really likes you, and it freaks him out!

Mar

For three whole months we weren't ever quite a couple. We had email and text exchanges that stressed me out. I tried to not worry about him not inviting me to hang out when he knew my kids were with their dad and I was available, I tried to make plans. But almost inevitably he would end up calling me on Friday or Saturday nights, wanting to see me when I was home alone. I generally tried to have plans so I could at least send him the signal that he needed to ask in advance. But the truth was, I usually didn't have anything going on and I was weak. I would relent and see him last minute, feeling like a backup plan because nothing more fun had come up for him. It was confusing and dissatisfying.

Somehow we never returned to our first two magic dates. I invited him twice more to meet me for lunch and once more to come over for dinner - basically all I could do since I had three small boys running around and I didn't want to neglect them. But he was just a little aloof, he always ignored my invitations, as if I hadn't even asked him. Then he wouldn't invite me to do anything either, or at least not until the last minute. And his emails seemed almost cold. And he wouldn't call me his girlfriend or talk about our relationship at all. If I ever hinted around about our shared future he just shrugged it off, like he didn't want to discuss it, then he would change the subject.

When we were together it was almost the same, minus when we were having sex - something I only had the will-power to withhold for three weeks. And though the sex was incredible and he seemed loving in the middle of it, he always acted disappointed somehow that I hadn't maintained my chastity. Mentioning more than once about a friend who had waited for sex until marriage, another friend who had married an "easy" girl who had jumped right in the sack with him. I felt terrible, like I'd proven myself a whore. A whore with no husband and three young kids. Ugh. Of course, being a whore might not be the worst thing a woman can be. Because now, years later as I mope around trying to figure out how to not be mentally ill (because, FUCK that! I am not mentally ill! Life is hard and sometimes we need time to get over the crap!) I have to think Dex was kind of a jerk to me. But, you know, I didn't always waste my time with him. Once, after we had been dating maybe 3 months, we had this juicy little morsel:

From: Dextrous (On A Popular Social Media Site)
To: Amanda (right there on her public space - for the Whole World to see!)
RE: Last Night

I went to lunch with Mike. Got your voice mail a few minutes ago. You're teaching about volcanos, huh?. I'm still trying to figure out this social media business. I hope it's OK to write to you this way. I like that picture you posted of the dinner we had!

I am glad things are going well. You have a busy schedule. I am thinking about having a bon fire the weekend after this one. The 18th. I want to cook briskets all day and bbq in the evening. Pretty much hang around the house cooking and sipping beer. I think it will be my divorce party too. Not going to call it that though. If it comes together I hope you come.

Ya know it's funny I have always liked the prospect of being a volcanologist. The thought of probing steaming holes for some unknown reasons causes a rise in my interest. And yes, streaming magma is a beautiful thing too. Even if it sprays all over and can be messy. A powerful eruption is always fun to watch and witness especially when nothing gets ruined and no one gets hurt. It's amazing how the steam vent holes get filled from the inside until it is full and overflowing.
One time on the discovery channel I saw the mouth or crater of the volcanoes fill with hot magma until it over flowed. Once the geothermal pressure subsided the mountain swallowed the

magma back down. The size of geological events is mind boggling. Millions of metric tons! Talking about volcanoes gets me excited.

We should do something this weekend I will give you a call. We don't have to get a baby sitter. I can come over after they go to bed with a movie? I will call you this evening. I am going to Mike's to make fishing weights. Sort of like craft party except we are melting lead and drinking beer.

Talk to you later
I hope you have a good afternoon at school.

DDD

From: TeacherAmanda@hometownmail.com (after quickly erasing his public message)
To: dexterousdoesit@engineeringfirm.com
Subject: Eruptions
September 15 at 2:55 PM

Why oh why do you tempt me into thinking about volcanic explosions? Pent up energy, pressure building, hard rocks blocking hot holes until the pressure gets too great and then there is an enormous and powerful explosion, shooting steaming magma into the sky? Really why? :) Tempering my passions is a fabulous test, sure to lead to a better life. Certainly.

So how has YOUR day been going? I've been really well. Super calm and feeling just fine about everything, amazingly. I've been working really hard to learn my yoga routine but I have to get special help with it today after school because I'm a slow learner. I'll get it eventually.

Thanks for the invites for this weekend. I'd really enjoy getting to see you, but my boys and I already have plans for lunch both Saturday and Sunday with my mom. How about the following Sunday, the 17th? Kinda far off but I've wanted to go to church with you guys. It would be nice to see you at another time, though. I could get a babysitter for this Friday or Saturday night if you want to do something. Let me know and I'll call the babysitter.

So, back to thinking of volcanoes and how they probably develop quite a bit of condensation before they finally release all that hot lava. (Oh -

and you might want to avoid posting personal things on social media, I know you're new to the whole thing…don't worry I erased it before our parents saw it!)

Amanda

Somehow I stuck it out for the rest of the winter, though. I just loved being with him, I loved how protected he made me feel, I loved how responsible and mature he was. But after three months of progressively colder and colder conversations I finally called him one night and ended it.

"Hello?" Dex answered his phone with his usual down-sounding greeting. Not the, hello?, with the voice going up in an opening question like most people use, but instead a, hello, with an Eeyoreesque downbeat.

"Hi Dex, it's me." I wanted to hear him be happy, to say Amanda! How good to hear from you. To put even the slightest bit of interest into his voice when he heard from me. But he never did. For three months he had been only friendly, as if I were just any person. Not a woman who hoped for a loving romance.

"Oh, hi." Was his response, again, as if Eeyore was on the other end.

I sighed. Here goes, I thought. "Dex, this is not working for me. I don't want to see you anymore."

He finally had a little emotion in his voice, "What? Did something happen?"

"No, no." I said, surprised he had responded so forcefully, almost like he cared. "I just don't feel like I am important to you."

He said, "How can you not think you are important to me? I see you whenever I have free time. I call you almost every night."

I sighed, "Yes, you call me. And you talk about your house, your wood stove, your latest engineering project, your truck…but I could be anyone. You never ask about me."

He got annoyed at this, "If you don't like what I talk about then tell me."

I didn't want to argue. "It's not just that," I said, trying to articulate why I wasn't happy. But somehow I didn't even know, it was just a feeling. I tried again, "You also haven't talked about us, as a couple, it's like we are going nowhere. I'm just some girl you are dating. I'm not even sure if I'm your girlfriend."

He was silent. I wondered if he was angry or sad or what. I was afraid he would hang up when I still didn't get a response after 30 seconds. "Are you still there?" I asked.

He sighed, and finally responded, "You are going though a lot right now. There has been no stability in your life for at least two yeara and it sounds like much of your marriage was unstable. A divorce is one of the biggest stressors to go through in life especially with kids. Give yourself a break. Don't put so much pressure on yourself to have all things in concrete so fast. If you did, the wrong things may be cast in stone. Allow yourself to breath and appreciate the life you currently have while aspiring for what you want."

This was quite the speech, and probably true, I should appreciate what I have. But he wasn't really responding to my issue, my issue of him not really committing. And he wasn't responding to what I said, I'd flat out said I wasn't sure if I was his girlfriend. And his response was that the wrong things might be cast in stone? I was confused. I didn't feel like this was going anywhere.

"Well," I said, "I guess you're right. I've had a pretty stressful year. I was hoping meeting you would be the start of something new and meaningful, but I guess it isn't going to work."

He softened, his voice over the phone was gentle as he said, "I'm sorry if I didn't do what you needed me to. I really like you. If your plans, schedule, and or anxiety do not allow for that then things will be as they are meant to be. If that is the case maybe we should set a date, for your sake, and evaluate where the relationship is at that point and make a decision then regarding where it is and is going? It could be a way to remedy your sense of limbo."

I felt even more scattered hearing this. Where was the emotion? Were we some merging business? I tried to think of some way to respond but he continued, "In either case, ultimately you have control of your life. You can choose to change your situation with regards to our relationship. You are not trapped in something that may not be what you need. I can try to do things that you need. I am not perfect for you. I may never be able to do well the things that you need. Or I may not be ready and able to support you emotionally right now. We are both still healing. Also, to set expectations based on romance novels and movies will be a sure recipe for shattered expectations. Or at least that is what I read some where."

I jumped in, "I am not basing this on a romantic movie! I just don't feel heard or like we have a stable relationship."

He chuckled, "Well, I know I like you, you are special to me and I will always care about you. Even if you aren't feeling like this will work."

I was shocked, hearing him say he likes me, I am special, he cares about me, surprised me. This is what I wanted all along. NOW he says it? Now that I'm trying to tell him I'm not happy? Why didn't he tell me this before I started to end it?

"You care about me?" I said in a small little voice, hating myself for being so needy.

"Of course I do, you are special to me," he said, I could just imagine his kind brown eyes crinkling up in a warm smile.

I was suddenly full of joy. I mattered to him! But his next words sent me back into my confusion and sadness, "But I understand that you need space to think about what we have, to see if we are really right for each other," he continued, "I think if you don't want to see me anymore then this should be what you do."

I felt like I was spinning, my thoughts were all clouded. Ten minutes before I had told him I didn't want to see him anymore, then he told me I was special to him and my dissatisfaction immediately disappeared. Now he was going back to us not seeing each other. I didn't even know how to respond, I felt I had made a big mistake somewhere in there but I didn't know how to fix it.

"Well, Dex, of course I still want to see you," I replied lamely. "I just want to know where we stand."

"I'm not sure what you are saying," he said, "I thought you wanted to break up. To not see me."

I felt my eyes fill with tears, as I said, "Well, I guess that is what I want. I need something more definite."

He sounded as sad as me as he agreed, "Yes, we need to do this right. I know I need someone who is the whole package, someone I can take to events. I want to be sure you and your kids will fit into my life. We need a break so we can know for sure."

My jaw dropped. Was he saying my kids and I are not the whole package? I didn't even want to talk to him anymore. I stuttered out a good-bye, then we said good-bye and hung up. And I burst into tears, crying into my pillow for most of the night.

Day 18

Now
Day 18

Tonight I'm going out, first time in over two weeks. I am going with my love to watch a concert.

The concert is pretty amazing. I am watching a lovely trio of three sisters, called 'Joseph' who play guitar and harmonize and sing pure poetry. We met them at a small event before their concert where we got to hear about their dreams of being musicians come to life. Really inspiring. Yet it also makes me feel an embarrassing twinge of despair. These young girls are so beautiful and talented, they have such potential and are pursuing their dreams. They play music and travel and are achieving what they set out to do.

I can't help selfishly thinking of my own situation. How did I let my dreams go? Why did I not trust my passions? Why was I always compelled to quietly take the safe route, never admit I had other goals for my life. Is it too late?

But more importantly: I need to BE HERE now. I am at this concert. I am here. Sitting here reflecting on my own life? At a concert? Ugh, I can't stand myself sometimes. I need to hear this music mixed together with the sound of a fierce rain on the tin roof. Listen to these girls, "I almost cut down my own tree. Sadness carved out a place for my joy." Exactly.

Day 19

Day 19

I could barely handle that small social event last night, though it was a wonderful concert. Too loud, too many complicated people, too much everything. Is it possible I've hidden my total fear of social situations all this time...by being drunk? Maybe. People are too much trouble. It's so much easier away from them. I wish my love could more understanding and helpful. Or maybe he is and I'm just really needy.

I need supportive people around me. Not people like the relative-by-marriage who I ran into at the grocery store. She asked me, as if she cared, "How ARE you, Amanda?" Then didn't acknowledge when I told her I was healing. I guess that makes since. She is also an ex-drinker. I tried to tell her how I was struggling to be in big social situations. She did not reply, instead she asked about my job, told me she had "heard" I was quitting. Before I could even explain she continued on, saying "people" are lucky to have jobs and shouldn't ask too much of their employers. Then she walked away. No other word. Thanks relative who told her about my struggles. Thank you for sharing my life with your wife.

After our brief and painful "conversation" I had to remove myself and get calm, remind myself that she has her own struggles, her own worries. I can't take it personally. Her own kids stress me out with all their problems, I can't imagine how she deals with them. I need to remember that, with this woman, any time she asks me a question about my life and actually manages to elicit information from me, then she immediately cuts me down.

While wrinkling her nose. This is her problem, not mine. Don't tell her anything. Ever.

Day 20: Clinging to the Edge

Day 20:

Still on that good 'ol path to better, right? Right!!!???

Today was the 20th day of overcoming the terrible path I was on. I woke up at 5:15 in the morning feeling pretty good, in fact it occurred to me that if I jumped out of bed I could get to the 5:30 yoga class at the Y…but did I? Oh no, instead I made the shit choice to grab my phone off of my bedside table (what a stupid place to keep a phone/computer) and get totally sucked into my virtual world. I read emails, I don't even remember what they were they were so irrelevant. Probably the same marketing, buy this wallpaper you looked at once, buy this tiny computer you looked at another time!! from Amazon. Not to mention re-visiting the emails from work (oneweekoneweekoneweek) reminding me to fill out forms for my absence, and would I like to request a new assignment?, and don't forget our meeting where we want to see all of your medical information for the past 39 years. Oh yes, and I also got bogged down in the Facebook quagmire - don't forget the eyelash event! The fingernail event! The clothing sale event! Plus the requisite brags about kids and job success and parties, just in case my self-esteem might have needed one more little nudge into the dark.

Info overload complete, I tried to return to sleep. Why? My love and the kids were both peacefully silent, sleeping, so I thought a few more minutes would be useful. Of course, my mind started churning about my career, the failure and shame and injustice of it. The inevitable return next week complete with questions from well-meaning strangers - er, I mean coworkers and kids. The horrible classroom environment, the rude secretary who seems hell-bent on destroying me, the kids who come from such horrible circumstances they can't help but let it seep into all their interactions. Not to mention the administration that ignores me and sees me as a problem, not an asset. The colleagues who declare their expertise so loudly, even though they really, really, do not know what they are talking about. Really. Just because their parents paid for them to go to an expensive private school and their husbands are rich and teaching is just a fun hobby for them. This does not give them a genuine understanding of how the language department should be run. And all that. Running between my ears and creating a headache around my forehead and down to my brainstem in an endless loop.

I closed my eyes firmly, trying to sleep or get the pain to go away. Arching my back in agony over my failed career - so amazing ten years ago! I was so valued the superintendent and my principal came into my classroom and asked me to be a principal! But I was too scared to jump on that chance. I was so amazing they put my cute picture on the wall of the board room. I was so qualified and incredible and such a great leader they gave me a plaque at a district-wide event. Where did that girl go? What happened to her? How can that girl turn into a woman who is now shuffled around, assignment to assignment, the worst windowless classroom spaces at the farthest ends of the building (or not even IN the building), no teaching partner, no curriculum, the kids with the most trauma and behavior problems. How can that happen to a person's career? Even now typing this I start to cry, because I think I know. I believe I know what happened: I couldn't handle the agony of my personal life and it bled into my career, destroying my abilities.

From the moment the police came, seven years ago, and arrested my husband for beating me up in the front yard of our beautiful home in a fancy neighborhood my life ended. Obviously. Like someone can continue on after that…not with an infant and two toddlers and suddenly homeless. How can someone keep being a shining star at work with that shit? But, you know, that was seven years ago. I should have been able to recuperate. To bounce back. To show some grit and perseverance. But somehow I didn't. Somehow I made bad decisions and cried at work and wrote and wrote and wrote in a journal instead of, like, teaching or leading or paying attention at meetings. I just didn't bounce back very well. So they transferred me. If I hadn't had a union they would have fired me, right? Then I might have woken up. But instead I went to a new place and blundered around feeling suddenly unimportant and useless and invisible. My voice stripped and my abilities unseen.

And made more bad decisions. Like getting shit-faced drunk every time the state made me send my tiny babies, still in diapers, to be alone with the violent man who promised he would hunt me down and kill me. Pacing my tiny apartment, stumbling, as I guzzled wine, trying not to think about how scared I was. Nope, I should have figured out a better way. I should have talked to someone. But all my friends were happily married with husbands that were kind to them, husbands who didn't hold knives over his head while yelling, "Die, bitch, die!" while the babies slept next door. They didn't want to hear my stupid sobbing. My parents tried to help me, they invited us to dinner twice a week - good thing, too, since he never paid child support and food was hard to pay for. But my family was as devastated by my sudden failure as I was. Their "Perfect Child" had not only stumbled, she had plunged into a oily pit, dragging her three tiny babies with her.

So needless to say, my career might not have been my top priority. But I did my best. I tried. I certainly did a good job at the aspects I could control - the planning, management, instruction - I can take solace in the fact that I did not let my students down. I always kept a happy face on and got good reviews from evaluators. I always did what I was supposed to. If I have any true skill in this life it is listening to what people tell me to do and then doing it. I am a good follower.

So here I am, lying in bed, hearing the first morning birds tweet and my love's steady breathing and seeing the gray dawn grow, tears again streaming down my face. I reached for the damn phone again (god I hate that fucker. I was so much healthier before that thing invaded my life) and opened the HappySpace app that seems like maybe a good way to get my mind back on track.

And it did, actually, I read a meditation exercise: deep breathing, send good blessings first to myself, then to a loved one (my love and the kids), then to an acquaintance, then to someone you are angry at.

I'm not sure how far I got because I fell asleep. That might have been good, I guess, but then in my very short last-minute sleep I had a nightmare about people in the woods. Big dumb dinosaurs (hey! That's what we used to call old, useless teachers! Hmmm....) crashing around. A captured wolf. A dog sniffing the dinosaurs. People lost.

Needless to say, the rest of the day was off. Not terrible. I did everything I could to hold on, to cling to my health. I listened to an uplifting TED Radio Hour about a guy who chose to live a year Biblically. I meditated. I drank juice, not the wine my love left sitting, open, on the counter (in fact I moved the stupid bottle into the basement because it was calling to me). I played Monopoly with Cody, Winston, and Sam. But I felt really low all day.

Starting the day off right seems like an important thing to do. Maybe even vital.

Day 21: Starting the Day Off Right

Day 21

Though it's only 9:30 in the morning and I have already cried pretty heart wrenchingly once today, I know today will be a better day. Even if I do have to take the kids to see their dad and Cody cried and said he's afraid to go. I told Cody to call 9-1-1 if his dad starts to lose his temper. I helped Cody memorize the address of his dad's house. Please God let them be OK these next three days.

Last night, before bed, I bawled and bawled. My love held my hand and just listened as I sobbed, barely understandable, telling him how scared I am to send my kids to my ex-husband. How all these years I've just buried that terrible fear with going immediately over to Penny's or Maria's or just to a bar alone if my friends weren't around. Then just getting so numb with pot and beer or wine that I couldn't feel anything at all for two full days. Laughing and smoking and checked out, refusing to think about the reality I couldn't face. And now, it's bubbling up, now after all these years of avoiding the pain, it is going to be inevitable. There is absolutely nothing I can do except ride it out. Feel the pain.

Covering it up with anti-depressants and anti-anxiety pills coupled with all the legal crap I could invest as fast as possible whenever the hurt started to arrive wasn't really working for me anymore. Those "helpers" were not really helping me, not if I want to be here for the long game. So here I go. Here's the long game.

Today I woke up at 5:15 again, because - hey! Guess what? That's what time I wake up when I go to sleep sober at ten at night. It's actually a really good time to wake up. And instead of reaching for the piece of shit smart phone and immediately getting bogged down in the world, instead I got out of bed, grabbed a really useful book called 'Instant Emotional Healing' and went into the living room. I turned on the pretty white lights and the fireplace and I followed the directions in the book for the acupressure and tapping meditations and felt pretty good. Then I returned to bed, maybe I should have taken the dog on a walk or something, but it was still dark. I fell asleep again for maybe twenty minutes, but I didn't have a nightmare.

After making the kids breakfast I went to the Y. I didn't really feel like going, but I've discovered this, like meditation and not wallowing in bed with my phone, helps me tremendously for the rest of the day. So I marched around on the treadmill while listening to cheerful music and I felt pretty good.

This recovery thing, this overcoming depression and addiction and the crap that caused

depression and addiction is a slow, long process.
And if I can start my day out right I just might
heal. Plus I guess maybe I should examen some of
that crap I've been hiding from all this time.

Dealing with Old Suffereing
as a Way to Heal

With Dex, was I afraid of getting close to someone else? Is this why I created such impossible standards? Was I afraid I was the problem? That if I loved again, married again - bad things could happen again? I'm too messy? I'm too outspoken? Or something inside me incites rage? Why wouldn't it, after my marriage. Ten years? All that bullshit for ten years? Then all that MORE bullshit for four more years with Dex. Of course I am mad at myself, at my inability to let go of things that don't work. Like my stupid job, all these many years into it. I'm looking at nearly twenty years as a teacher and it is not getting any better there either. It's not a love story, it's my career, I know. But a career should be a bit of a love story, right? If it's going to be a good career. Not like some accident that you can't walk away from.

But maybe it's time to think about Will. Because all of this seems to stem from that trauma. And just drowning it in pharmaceuticals and fun times with friends doesn't really seem to be doing the trick, does it?

The anniversary of one of our last fights is approaching - it was Valentines Day. I had planned a special dinner for Will. He had worked late that night, he had school conferences. It was after 8:00 when he got home and Cody and Sam were already sleeping. I was six months pregnant with Winston. I was happy to see him, he'd been very attentive and sweet that morning. We'd brought both boys in to bed with us and he had said to me, "Look, we make a heart and our kids are inside."

But when Will got home, he didn't walk all the way inside. He just stood in the doorway, asked about my plans for that evening. I said dinner waswaiting in the oven, his favorite, lasagne. But I could tell he wanted to leave, probably to go smoke pot and go to the bar - or whatever he was going to say he was doing. I suspected even then that he wasn't being faithful, but I just wanted everything to be OK. He was irritated and wanted to leave, no matter what I said or did. He had purchased a bag of weed the night before and he had that restless almost-action about him.

But he probably felt guilty or obligated to stay home because I tended to pout when he left us - which happened every day, all day. Or maybe he just wanted to fight. Because when I told him I had made lasagne he just rolled his eyes and walked away. I followed him out into the kitchen and started to pull dinner out of the oven. I asked Will to ask one of his colleague's about hew childcare situation. Even though Winston wasn't born yet, I was preparing for my baby, trying to find someone to watch him the next fall. I was calm, cheerful - just taking care of family business.

Will instantly changed. He went from being fairly quiet to furious. He stomped to the counter and wiped it with a sponge saying "Why are there crumbs all over the counter?"

Then he shouted, "You are the WORST FUCKING HOUSE KEEPER!"

My face flushed red. That made me mad! He was so unfair, so unsatisfied, so anal about our house. Yet - I had spent a pleasant afternoon outside, watching our boys play in the unusually nice February sun. So I felt guilty, because it was true, while he was at his school conferences, I had been having a nice afternoon. So I erupted, angry! I stood up and yelled about how hard it was to take care of two babies and do housework and have a full time job. I stomped into the family room and started furiously picking up toys. He just followed behind me, watching, like he always did. To make sure I did a good job. I was so pissed I started asking him what he was doing, why was he watching me?..... and that's when things got bad.

But I can't tell that story right now. Even if it was years ago, it still upsets me to thing about it. Maybe this is part of the appeal of Dex, he was a good distraction. Just like Carlisle was a good distraction before I started dating Dex. Distraction is what keeps me from panicking about Will.

Long Ago,

Many Years Ago

I was the first in my family to attend college,
though my lack of experience made the experience
difficult for me. I arrived in Portland, Oregon
ready to begin college at 18 years old. I had
decided to live off campus, simply a poor decision
made by me and my parents because we had NO
CLUE. Amazing how having no prior experience
will make life just that much more difficult. Since,
no one in my family had ever gone away to college
before no one knew what the heck we were doing.

I stumbled around the administration building with my dad, trying to figure out how best to get registered and into classes. My mom hadn't come with us. She was still angry at me for choosing to spend my senior year of high school in Mexico as an exchange student. But that's a story not even worth thinking about.

I sigh now as I look back on my life. So much potential. I was really going places in college. Many professors pulled me aside to tell me what a strong student I was, to encourage me to do big things. But did I? No, I worried about failing. I partied. I got involved with Will. I wasted so much time and energy on a man who didn't encourage me or even support me. I wasted even more time covering up of feelings, pushing any negative thought or idea away, just letting everything pile up and around me until it finally broke.

So many things in my past seemed to weigh down on me, big decisions and small.

In college I had always taken as many courses as were allowed to take in one term (hey, it's the same price if you take 12 credits or 18, so you might as well take 18, right?!!) and I moved into a shockingly cheap studio apartment in downtown Portland, ensuring not just extreme overwork but also complete and utter isolation and no chance of meeting any friends. I had no idea how to cook anything other than chocolate chip cookies, so on top of being at school or doing homework or research 12 hours a day I also had to learn how to cook for myself. Somehow I managed to master pasta with garlic, yogurt with granola, and fried eggs. Eventually I remembered I also knew how to bake bread. I learned I could manage my stress a little bit by pulling myself away from my frantic studies to punch down and knead bread. I managed to attend Portland State University for three months and make almost no friends. Thankfully, that was when Erica Princeton and her band showed up. You might know who Erica Princeton is, right? If you have ever listened to Top 40 music you would, she played with the band, Flying Foes, for years - until one of the band members (and our friend) died. That's another tragedy I'm not quite ready to deal with.

I had been friends with Erica in elementary school, she had been in my brother Charlie's class and my close friend, Geri's neighbor. I knew her in that small town way, from many different people and past events. My brother Charlie had always liked her and whenever he came to visit me in Portland he contrived some way to be at the same party as Erica. I think Erica liked Charlie, too, she always lit up when he was around.

Erica's sister Penny has been my close friend since high school. Our luck with men is sadly similar, but having a friend to commiserate with was nice. Penny had invited me to a party the summer before and Erica was there. While we were catching up Erica had told me she was thinking about moving to Portland with her new band. That fall in Portland Erica called me and my life of perfection and focus opened up into one of fun. I began to meet new people and go out on occasion and relax a little bit. Now, this is not to say I stopped focusing so much on my 4.0 or being the perfect student, not at all. Just that my down time included a little more than just baking bread or riding a bike.

Now, years later, I think about that winter and spring when I had been so busy with Erica and her exciting life. I remembered the first time Erica invited me to a party at Carlisle's house. Carlisle played the drums with the Flying Foes, but that wasn't what mattered to me. HE mattered to me, just as him. Not that I'd ever had the guts to tell him. At that time, he lived with three guys, Tom, Dax, and Al in a duplex a few blocks from school. I was nervous because I hadn't seen Carlisle since choir in high school and I'd always had kind of a crush on him. Also, I had not really spent much time at parties, yes in discos when I had spent ten months in Mexico while in high school, but there I had been more of a spectacle than a participant. And discos in Guadalajara Mexico were the height of elegance and this was, well, not elegant. At all.

These four young men lived about how you would imagine four young men would live, but way worse. It was horrible. Dishes, dirty laundry, a filthy floor, and eeeeek! A centerfold picture tacked to the wall. Granted she was modestly covered because it was a 1970's Playboy Centerfold, but still. My innocent eyes were as big as saucers. Erica laughed, pulling me further inside as she confidently called to her bandmate and his friends. That horrible, sleazy house full of scary men soon felt comfortable and Al, Dax, and Tom became some of my favorite people. This is where I learned to have fun. I even dated Al a little, though we both knew it wasn't going anywhere. Carlisle was rarely around, he was studying music at the University and spent any free time practicing his drum either alone in his basement bedroom or with the Flying Foes to prepare for their ever more numerous gigs.

The first few weeks I sat primly on the couch waiting for Erica as she practiced for upcoming concerts, but one day Carlisle showed up. Even though I knew him slightly from high school, Carlisle was the most terrifying of all to me. A few people on campus called him Jesus because, quite simply, he looked like Jesus: tall, thin, and pale with long dark hair. Carlisle was somehow really scary because he wore this tough-looking black motorcycle jacket and had this slow deliberate walk. I had watched him even in high school and I had always felt nervous of him, like he might be the kind of guy my mom warned me to stay away from. But I was drawn to him too, I had always wanted to talk to him.

I remembered that warm fall day when Carlisle approached me.

"Hi." He said, smiling down at me where I sat going through note cards, preparing for a test.

"Hi." I squeaked.

"You're Amanda, right? I remember you from back home. Erica told me she was going to bring you to the party tonight."

I nodded dumbly.

Eventually Carlisle was able to draw me out of my terrified shell by asking me about my classes and family. He was soft spoken and kind and not in the least bit tough, his exterior was absolutely not an accurate depiction of his personality.

It was then that I was able to start joining these light-hearted college kids and have fun, in moderation of course, when all of my other work was done. In fact, it was a huge relief to have a social outlet when I had free time. I was able to laugh and relax and learn about people and make friends. I started drinking beer and smoking pot. Of course, being responsible Amanda, I was often the one at the party making sure everyone had finished their homework or helping people finish their papers that they had procrastinated on. My friends would pay me to help them write papers, sometimes with cash but often with a bag of weed or a six-pack of dark beer. I would sit at the computer and direct them as they struggled to write, asking them if they thought an introduction might be a good idea or a quotation.

But it was Carlisle I enjoyed the most. For a few months we had been inseparable, sharing jokes and a love of music. Though we were never anything more than friends. Not that I wasn't interested…Carlisle had been the first guy who had ever kissed me THAT way, though we had never done more.

THAT kiss happened that spring, at a party towards the end of the school year. I was standing in a large group debating whether Donald Duck or

Daffy Duck was a better character when I felt a tap on my shoulder. I turned around to find myself facing my friend Carlisle.

He hadn't said a word, only tilted my chin up, leaning down and kissing me tenderly on the lips. For a long time. When he was done he had simply walked away leaving me gaping as our friends teased me. But after that neither one of us had been able to take it any further. Carlisle was always so sincere and honest and kind to me and we continued to spend time together as friends. But we were both shy, even though I like to think he loved me, even back then.

But only a few months later, Carlisle and Amanda and their band mates, Jimmy and Ben had moved to Los Angeles. It was weird for us to watch our friends get more and more popular, but The Flying Foes had signed a major record deal in Los Angeles. I had fun hearing about them, living vicariously through their success, but it wasn't long before we never really heard from them at all - they had moved on to another world.

A casual friend, May, from my Western Civilization class had a guy she wanted me to meet: Will. Really, May liked Will's friend Rand, so Will and I were more of an afterthought. But May arranged for the four of us to have a double date. Will and I hit it off like hotcakes on a griddle, which is to say perfectly but really shouldn't stick together too long. He was not a stranger to me, I had attended a student-designed class he and his good friend Bobby had put on the previous spring called Great Film Directors and he had seemed interesting. Actually, he had seemed cocky and his close-together eyes gave him a suspicious ratty look, but hindsight is 20-20, right?

Will ended up being in my Geography 305 class. I'm not saying we were in the same class, but that he was in my class, because I was a conscientious student and he skated by, barely attending class at all. The first day of class I arrived 15 minutes early so I could ensure the best seat (and, I believed, the highest grade) front and center. By the time class had started no one had sat next to me, so when Will sauntered in five minutes late Dr. Levy hollered out, "Here's a seat here, right next to this young lady." Well, charmer that he was, Will ended up with my phone number by the end of the class and with my heart by the end of the term. I nearly forgot all about Carlisle at this point, although being with Will was less than perfect.

Time marched on. The Flying Foes became more and more popular and soon I never saw Carlisle and rarely saw Erica though she and I occasionally exchanged emails and holiday visits. I read about Carlisle in magazines and soon felt too shy to even try to contact him. My brother, Charlie even stopped talking about Erica after awhile. Then he met Rachel while working in our hometown and they soon settled down. Our youth passed by and we all grew up.

Being with Will wasn't all bad, by any means. But it certainly wasn't all good. Somehow all those days of fun came to an end, never to be found again. Sure, in fleeting moments: a Saturday night with friends, a lunchtime laugh with colleagues, an exuberant breakfast with family. But that tiny window of time when I was young and free and surrounded by people who were having just as much fun as me was something I would treasure, yes, but also just painfully miss.

Maybe that's why I married Will. I just missed it all and he was my boyfriend, not even a boyfriend who treated me all that well, but my boyfriend through it nonetheless. He was the guy I would show up with at the parties or meet after class or talk to about finals. So we got married. And now, seventeen years later, all I have to show for Will are three really amazing children and a monthly notice from the state saying Will owes me a ton of money.

Not All

Years Ago

I look back at my life and sometimes it just seems like, if I could have just stayed away from me (except for of course just long enough to have my babies with Will), then maybe I would have had a totally different life. Though, really, not all the men in my life were a waste of time. I have to remember that the one person who stood out the most for me through it all was Carlisle. And my feelings for Carlisle didn't just end completely, even after I met Will and we moved back to my hometown. My mental health probably would be better if they had. But after that brief fun time in Portland before he was famous, I saw him a couple more times back home.

Today I thought about that fateful meeting and I dug out the beginning of obsessive writing about Carlisle - I wisely burned most of it because I really don't want anyone to know just how crazy I can be at times and that shit was crazy. I was still married when I wrote this, in fact Will and I hadn't even had kids yet. But somehow, even though it was many years ago, I still continued to think about one small moment in time:

Many Years Ago: Saturday, 3 am

Ohhhh my God, I am in rapture. Shit. Carlisle...he's back home! I've always loved him, since we were in high school and he would tease me about always being the first person to raise my hand in class. And I loved him even more when he was at Portland State, studying music.

But I couldn't believe when I walked into The Pear last night, he was there! I hadn't seen him in years and my heart just leapt. Erica was in town visiting her sister Penny and we met up with Maria and Geri. Crap, I kind of abandoned them. OK, I totally abandoned them. I need to call them.

But back to Carlisle. He was the first person I saw when I walked in. Carlisle, standing in the middle of the room. He's tall and ten times more handsome than when we were in school - not that it matters because I have always loved him. But I walked up to him, said hi, chit-chatted, all the normal crap. Walked away....and couldn't stay away. I wanted to talk to him a couple more times and always got caught up with someone else. Then as Erica, Geri, Penny, Maria, and I were standing near him these two asshole guys I've never seen before started to fight. Of course, Carlisle, valiant guy that he is, tried to pull them apart and I poured my beer on them. As the fight was breaking up, I pointed out that he had blood on his shirt. Wow, he took it off and just wore his undershirt and he is so gorgeous.

We talked for a bit, and I could tell he was as into me as I was into him. I was really brave, finally! I told him how much I've always liked him, how much I'd loved that surprise kiss back in college. He laughed at that and then blushed, saying he'd liked it too. Then I asked him to walk with me. He agreed readily and followed me out the door. We walked around outside, held hands, silly banter. Then we sat on the steps of the college and talked. We talked about everything, even politics and religion - of course we are still similar. The we walked back to The Pear, but we didn't go inside. I made him sing that nerdy song from choir, we held hands and he twirled me around and he was so sweet and kind. It was cold and he invited me to sit in his car. He drove for about a minute and he wanted to take me home. Shit. So I said no and refused. I didn't mention that Will and I were still married, even though I wasn't even living with him at that time - I tried, unsuccessfully, to leave Will many times during our marriage. I never even thought about Will, I was too absorbed by Carlisle. Then he asked me what I wanted to do and I realized I wanted to pull over and kiss him. I couldn't say it but my silence was enough. I made sure I wouldn't be tempted to see him again, that he was leaving and wouldn't be around. Then I said that what I really wanted to do was kiss him.

He pulled over in about three seconds flat and I turned and kissed him. It was soooooo nice. We kissed and kissed and kissed for over an hour. I leaned against him and he played with my hair and sang along to the radio. He just sat calm and still, holding me for so long. He would look at me, kiss me gently and stroke my hair. Incredible. Never, never have I been with someone and felt such tenderness. And we didn't even have sex.

After awhile he dropped me off at my house and we started to kiss again and I realized I could just spend all night with him. But then reality set in and before I could change my mind I told him he needed to go. When I opened the door he said he would like to get together. Damn! Why'd he have to end up being so perfect?

But of course, is anything that perfect and easy? The next morning I got a few texts:

_____

From: Erica
To: Amanda
9 am

So....you and Carlisle!! He's so much nicer than Will! I'm glad your divorce is final. C was over the moon this morning. I want the juicy dish lady. Hooray! E

From: Carlisle
To: Amanda
9:07 am

I found out you're married.

From: Erica
To: Amanda
9:17 am

Oh God. I'm sorry. I thought your divorce was final. Please forgive me. Talk to Carlisle, he's upset.

And That Was That

Many Years Ago

I didn't see or hear hardly anything more from
Carlisle. Not that I didn't want to, who wouldn't
after that? After that one cryptic text I tried to call
him, but he didn't even answer. I left some
pathetic blubbering voicemail about how I had
been unhappy for a long time, mean ol' Will blah
blah blah. I probably just sounded like a desperate
and amoral nut. No wonder he never called me
back. I even tried to see him, I knew he was only
here for one more day and I drove around like

some crazy stalker trying to figure out where he was. But of course I never saw him. I ended up getting sucked back into Will's world, letting him move back in, sticking it out for years.

Erica felt terrible, but being me I didn't tell her what was going on until months later. Neither did Carlisle. She told me later she figured we were both just being private and she hadn't wanted to be too nosy. Not to mention I think she was stressing about some LA executive dipshit. Whatever the circumstances, once again I let Carlisle just fade out of my life. Not necessarily out of my head, mind you, just my life. I still thought about him all the time. But at that time I was caught up in a rocky marriage and I just didn't see a way out. Rekindling an old romance, no matter how lovely and important to me, just wasn't something I was able to do.

So I just entertained myself with playing the night over and over in my head. And following Carlisle and his band as they got more and more famous. The Flying Foes. Though I didn't tell anyone I was obsessively reading everything I could about The Foes, even my brother, Charlie.

He and I had seen them as often as we could in Portland, my big brother had been one of their biggest fan. But he never even mentioned them once he married Rachel, I think she was probably jealous. I figured he had finally moved on. Like I needed to.

I thought I might have forgotten about Carlisle if his picture hadn't appeared about a year later in that magazine holding hands with Simone. As in SIMONE. The model. The stupid magazine was right there at the grocery store, claiming he was planning his proposal. Married? I couldn't believe I just let that guy walk away, I realized. I wondered if maybe I had always loved him.

His possible marriage loomed over me, even though I never said a word about it to anyone. He even brought Simone home to visit and I ran into them downtown. Ah, I thought I was over him then, I did - I refused to talk to him beyond a curt hello. I wanted to show him I had moved on.

And since it looked like Carlisle and the fabulous Simone were getting serious, I was finally able to move on too. Not that Will was really a great method, he gave me more stress than anyone else, but we managed to have three beautiful boys. Later, after we divorced, I still thought about Carlisle on occasion. But I figured Dex was a good fit, though I was pretty unhappy with him too. And Dex was always so and unstable, sometimes it felt worse than dealing with Will's temper. At least I knew Will loved me. Too bad Will's love was so psycho and explosive and jealous. I guess Dex just seemed like a good alternative to Will, maybe that's why I stuck with him even though I knew it was going nowhere.

Leagues

Geri and I went to lunch and we returned to our recent topic - what makes someone "in your league?" I guess I don't really know - is it the crowd you fit into? Dating someone who is the same social class, education level, intelligence, and looks? Carlisle used to be just right for me, but now he's dating a supermodel. Not to mention he's the drummer for The Flying Foes. So, obviously, he's completely out of my league.

What about Dex? Were we each other's leagues? I think it is odd that Dexterous once told me I'm out of his league, I wonder why?

I just know that in my life I've never really felt like I fit into a lot of crowds though I sort of fit into all. In high school I was pretty much a theatre nerd except there weren't many other theatre nerds. I dressed weird, was interested in bizarre ideas and activities, partied...but also got good grades, went to church, and was polite to adults. Plus I was friendly to everyone, especially people that no one else would talk to - which pretty much sealed my fate as uncool.

In college I sort of found my niche - I was a partier/super student. Truly, I found my calling for awhile there - all the guys were so impressed at my stamina for drinking Henry's beer. Yep. I still dressed really weird - which was no longer considered weird because somehow by that point I guess I was pretty. And being weird and ugly is not OK, but being weird and cute is cool. Though I still felt the same inside - pretty is temporary, not just as time goes on, but as a day goes on. But besides partying I had my little perfect double life

- education major with a 4.0 GPA, campus tour guide, Spanish tutor, still polite and fairly conservative looking. So in the end I didn't fit into either group, not really a partier, not really a good girl and I continued my quest to find people like me. Random and genuine with a mixture of good and bad. Carlisle was this to a T, I loved how he always got me.

Then as a young adult, things got even harder. High school teacher by day, beer drinking pool player, actress, and dancer at night. Of course, never sleeping made this all possible, but I was like two people - two people who wouldn't even like each other if they could meet. I was such an incongruous dichotomy, the little jumper dresses and glasses all laid out next to the penny loafers ready for the ninth graders next to the crumpled black hip-hugger jeans and knee-high black leather boots. In the morning the superintendent of our large district visiting my perfectly organized and managed classroom to try to promote me to principal; in the evening making out with a cute drummer outside a bar.

So what is my league? Now, I don't even want to think about it because I am still these two different people. Really truly I am a good woman, a gentle and kind teacher and mom who just happens to drink and dance and converse with lots of people on the few nights a month when my kids are with their dad. So is a decent and respectable guy my league? A man who, like me, goes to work every day and does a good job and is liked and respected by the community? Yes, of course this is my league. And how about a man who is also a lot of fun and enjoys drinking beer and singing karaoke and telling jokes? Well, yes - though it is hard to find a person who can pull off both of these. Then add to that the way I look which I believe might turn some people away because I teach yoga and have long blonde hair and model for the local tourism commission. It's hard because my league might seem like it should be some handsome slick'em guy, but I've never trusted attractive men.

But I remember oce Maria told me the Town Gossip had said Dexterous was still (still???) hung up on me but she said I am "out of his league." Why? What does that mean? He is educated, intelligent, has a good job, owns a home and property....what about that doesn't go with an educated, intelligent, professional woman? Unless you take into consideration that he is not an Adonis - but I used to love his extra weight. I though he was mmmm-mmmmm cute. Or is it the people he hangs around with? The Coors Light drinking, blue-collar, hometown folks he spends his free time with? My family is that way - though I'll admit I'm not. I think I've read too much, travelled to much, yet that is my original world. So back to the original question: what makes a person in your league?

Hidden Pain

Three(ish) Years Ago

Here's my thing: I only like assholes who hurt me. No. No, no, no - I need to tell myself what I WANT, right? Self-fulfilling prophesy and all that idea. Say what you want and it will come, we attract what we talk about, think about, etc. Cool I get that. But right here I need to wallow in pity because I have been resoundedly rejected (again) and my heart is, to paraphrase Kipling, stinging like a white hot brand. Damn it, Dex NEVER was consistent about calling me! Even when we ran into each other, had breakfast and a loving conversation, shared a passionate kiss on my front porch…then…nothing.

What hurts the most is it is not rejection of the uncontrollable surface aspects of my personality - you know, I'm ugly or fat or hard to get to know so they just don't give me a chance. That would be a tremendous consolation, really: he just didn't take the time to get to know me.

No, I have now been painfully rejected for the third time by the third man I've handed my aching heart to: Dex. Not some relative stranger but instead someone who truly knows me, has seen all I have to offer, has listened to my songs, met my family, learned my zany sense of humor, held me while I cried....and THEN decided, nah, no thanks - not for me. Yet again someone I have borne my soul to, someone I accepted completely, loved with my whole heart, trusted with my deepest feelings and ideas decided there is someone or something better. In fact, being alone is better than being with me.

There. Was that pitiful enough? Or shall I heap more negative depressing ideas on top of it? Because even when I tried to be so strong and end our relationship even when I knew it wouldn't work, I had somehow allowed Dex to suck me back in. I kept agreeing to see him and somehow three years passed.

I beat the shit out of myself even further - just like my ex-husband did for all those years. See, someone needed to take on the role of me-bashing, there is a vacancy and for lack of available assholes I'll just insult myself.

Pretty fucked up, huh?

Pretty scary that someone can be writing these things just before heading upstairs in this pretty high school where everyone wants to send their kids. I'm going to slap on a pretty, happy face and go teach ninth grade. And teach it really well. No one notices how sad I am.

What a great pretender. God help me.

And So It Dragged On

Reflections on the Past

When I got married at the way too young age of twenty my mom had tried to warn me that I was making a mistake, but had I listened? No way! My own parents had been divorced and I hadn't understood the difficulty or real value of marriage. I had dated Will for only my last year of college and when we graduated marriage had just seemed like the next step. I had just gotten my first teaching job, high school Spanish in my home town high school. Life just seemed like it had been trucking along great. I met Maria my first year, she was my teaching partner and she made the stress of the job bearable. At that time I felt like the smallest little things were huge, though I didn't really even have any problems. Except one, my husband. I have to roll my eyes at my naive young self. I had been so mistaken, thinking life was cut and dry and easy.

Will had a temper. I had noticed when we were dating, it would have been impossible to miss. But I just hadn't cared, we were having fun, we had a ton of friends and we were both successful and I had a plan and he was a part of it. His temper would flare up on occasion but it was only rarely directed at me. As the years had passed, however, things had gotten worse. Small insults had turned into daily name calling, threats of violence had turned into shoving which had turned into locking me in the bedroom and screaming at me all night as I cowered under a pillow. But I had continued on with my life, my seemingly perfect life, pretending nothing was wrong, not even telling Maria.

My brother Charlie started to question my safety, though, when I showed up at his house with the boys in the middle of the night after the Valentine's Day event.

"When did this happen?" Charlie had asked, pointing to the ugly purple bruise, a clear sign that I had been forcibly pulled by the upper arm.

Looking up at my big brother guiltily, I had considered lying. But he knew. He knew. Although our own dad was gentle and loving and we had never experienced any violence in our home, one of our cousins had lived with an abusive step-dad for a couple of years and it had affected everyone in the family. Just the stories were enough to give us nightmares when we had overheard the adults talking about it.

I hadn't even had to speak. I felt my eyes well up with tears, my chin wobbled, and with that small look, his four words, I knew my brother knew. Though it took me a few more months to really get a clue. Charlie had called my dad and my family had swirled to action around me, getting the story out, their concern and love finally allowing the torrent of fear and shame of years of mistreatment and belittling abuse to be revealed. The children played while I whispered of the bat kept in the closet, wielded over my face whenever he lost his temper. Of the sleepless nights while he paced the room screaming at me, refusing to allow me to sleep, threatening to kill me for something as small as not returning a library book on time.

By the time Will figured out where we had run, I was no longer there. He was furious at my dad and my brother when they calmly informed him that they would not allow him to hurt me, that he was not welcome in their family, and that his wife would be filing for divorce. Though he raged at them, blamed me, and made a big scene, he eventually accepted that this time screaming and scaring people would not get him his own way. Of course, being pregnant with Winston, so I had returned to Will. My family was shocked and angry with me, but Will eventually had talked me into returning. Less than a year later, though, things blew up again and I managed to get my three boys and myself out.

That was when we went to my Great Aunt Gloria's home where we lived in hiding for over a year while I waited for the divorce to be finalized. Sometimes I would get paranoid and we would all stay somewhere else. The kids didn't see Will at all for awhile. It was a nightmare, but one with an end, the end of not being mistreated any more. As one of the many counsellors I had spoken with reminded me, I didn't want my tiny sons to grow up thinking it was ok to treat their wives or girlfriends as poorly as their mom had been treated.

At first I felt I would not survive, living in the tiny guest room in Gloria's basement, sneaking the children to my step-mother to care for them while I went to work, always looking over my shoulder for Will. I was so fearful in the first few months that I hardly ate or slept. A couple of my friends, after crying with me, grieving and sympathizing, had consoled me that the baby weight was now gone. We tried to laugh about that one small solace. I was more thin than I had been even in high school, a fact I could hardly register so great was my grief. And grieve I did. Will may have been violent and unfair at times but he had also been my best friend and closest companion. His outbursts had been infrequent and if I could have overlooked them my life would have been perfect.

Afterward I was an outcast. Some of my friends, after listening raptly to my horrible tale, had abruptly disappeared, possibly afraid that my bad luck was contagious. I was sad to discover that I was now a third wheel, left out of many social occasions, no longer included where before Will and I would have been warmly welcomed. I listened, shocked at first, then resigned, as friends at work described Couples Bunco the weekend before, a camping trip, a birthday party. I was now on my own and no longer included. Only Maria and a couple of friends from childhood had stayed by my side at first.

This was about the time I ran into Carlisle again, downtown with Simone. It was just a couple of months before the divorce was final. When I look back, it is not at all surprising that I couldn't try to make something work with him at that time. I couldn't even hold it together for myself. It's a good thing I didn't try to pursue

Carlisle. If I had he probably would have turned out like Dex.

Worst of all at this time, though, was being a single mom. Single mom. Just the words sounded like a slur. At staff meetings other teachers would describe children that were troubled as kids with a "single mom" as in, you know, those kids with a single mom who can't stay out of trouble. Or that kid who has a single mom who doesn't show up for conferences. I just sat numbly, aware that my sweet innocent babies were now joining the ranks of underprivileged children. Despite my level of education and despite my love for them, they too were now children of a single mom.
Acquaintances on social media would joke about being a "single mom" for the weekend while their husbands went to a conference for the weekend. Oh! The horror of dealing with kids and a home without a husband for two days. I never commented on these insensitive posts, though I certainly could have.

And, as a single mom, I didn't have anyone to share the joy of my children with either. After we left Aunt Gloria's and I finally got my own apartment, I ate most meals alone with them, making toddler-esque conversations, dinosaur roars and big truck noises while I nursed the baby, wishing Will were there to see how cute they were. But Will was not there, in fact none of us had seen Will since that last evening when our lives erupted. He had called me once - to coldly inform me that he would "Find me and kill me" if I didn't come home to him. Then he had left me alone. He hadn't even shown up for our divorce court appointment, though he had hired a lawyer who bickered so much about every small possession (never the children, thank God) that the divorce took twice as long as it should have and left me with no home, no furniture, and no money - but I did have my kids. I had stood on the stand alone, thin and sad, simply stating that yes, I did want a divorce. When I left the courthouse I had felt slightly freer, though mainly just let down and disappointed. That night, after the kids had gone to sleep (at 7 pm, like they did every night at that point, leaving me alone with myself) I drank an entire bottle of champagne and lit our wedding candle outside on the patio, watching it burn down to the wick. I cried and laughed alone, drunk, before vomiting in my bushes. The next morning I

woke up ashamed and cleaned everything up
before the kids cheerfully woke up calling for me.

From that point on I vowed to make my life
better. Will had disappeared for a few months
managing to lose not only his wife and family but
also his job. I had to put the house on the market
and, with the extensive help of my family, had
gotten rid of almost everything and moved in with
Aunt Gloria then to a tiny apartment. I cried a lot.
I was really thankful for my job that paid me
enough to take care of my children but at the end
of every day I was exhausted and frazzled and
often felt like I was just barely keeping it together.

But the years passed and I did manage to keep
it together. I had a few friends that remained my
friend, Geri and Penny had been friends since
before high school and had loyally stood by me
even when a few others had not. They were true
friends, Geri and her husband Jason invited me and
my kids over for dinner once or twice a month,
even when the kids were small and a handful. Geri
and Jason had two children of their own, even
smaller and even more of a handful, so getting
together for a glass of wine and conversation was

something I always looked forward to. Maria was a wonderful friend too. Our work friendship had grown into weekly shared meals with our kids. I could always count on her.

Now, years later, I was content. The horrible divorce is something from the past. I decided a couple of years into it that I needed to change how I talked about the whole issue. I eventually got tired of being a victim, so now if anyone asked what happened or where Will went, I would just say he wasn't a good husband. That's it. No need to go into the rages or the infidelity that I always suspected but never proved. No need to tell all the terrible details. Now I am more focused on the future. Or at least trying.

One night, on a beautiful winter evening, Geri, Penny, Maria and I had more important issues to discuss than my floundering love-life, recipes, or children: our Halloween Party. We were going to have our annual kid-friendly but fun-for-adults party at Penny's. Or rather and Penny's parents house, better known as the Princeton Mansion. Penny was hoping her little sister Erica would be there too. We were all hoping she would, Erica is ridiculously famous and amazing since The Flying Foes got famous almost ten years ago. Like Carlisle, she is now so far out of everyone's league that we hardly ever see her anymore. But she is still our friend and we love to see her whenever we can.

Penny's ex-husband was a big waste, like Will, and she had always been a helpful friend. But Penny had a couple of things I didn't, number one being she was one of the richest people in town. Her dad is a famous Hollywood producer and her mom used to be a movie star. Sometimes I wonder how Penny could be so normal with so much wealth and fame surrounding her all the time. But she is. And we were all really excited about planing the party. I had tried to get them to include my friend Sonara, but both had shifted around uncomfortably when I mentioned her.

"What?" I asked, "you guys like her right?"

They both nodded, maybe a little too vigorously. "Sure, she's nice," Geri said. "She just dominates all the conversation."

"Yeah," Penny added, "and when we tried to plan that fund raiser with the book club she would only agree to her own ideas. She might be hard to work with."

I nodded, I understood. I really hadn't known Sonara that long. Her daughter was in my oldest son, Cody's, class at school.

By the time the evening was winding down with kids running in circles too tired to even want to play we had decided we needed a ladies' night out. My boys were going with Will the next evening (yes, after a year of counseling Will had gotten his life in order well enough to be able to have supervised visits then eventually weekend visits with the kids. I try not to freak out too bad when they are gone visiting him.) Penny didn't need to remind us that her live-in nanny would be watching her two boys. Geri's parents were taking her children for the evening, too, so she and Jason could have a "date night" though they were both eager to share their date night with friends. Geri didn't need to mention that going out alone with Jason was really boring. We are her friends and friends understand - that's the price you pay for a good solid husband sometimes.

And On...

Two(ish) Years Ago: Summer

I dredged up this fabulous morsel from the dark
pain of my mind. Ah, Dex, I am so glad you are
out of my life for good. Not that I don't
sometimes think of you. But a relationship that
never reaches a point of commitment is
exhausting. Especially for a woman who is alone
with three tiny children. Who has time for a man
who is always thinking there might be someone
more suitable for him…maybe…or maybe not…I
wish I had been able to just walk away. We dated

on and off for over three years! We struggled so much to stay together, but it just never worked.

How could I ever forget the time when he was supposed to go on a bike ride with all of us: the kids, my dad, a whole bunch of my friends (they should be his friends too, right? But he didn't hang out with me so they weren't his friends). But he never showed up at my house, just didn't appear. I didn't bother calling, why? After all the crap, why should I be the simpering fool who has to remind him when less than 24 hours before I had invited him and he had said yes. Why should I have to call him twice?

So my dad came, got all the bike stuff loaded, the trailers and blankets and kid helmets and everything, and we drove down to the park where we were all meeting up. It was so fun! These are my people. Not Dex's stupid friends that are always complaining about people who are weird and who won't recycle and who would never in a million years dress up for a Black-and-White themed bike ride. I was all decked out in my black jeans and white sweatshirt and the kids had on their black sweaters and even my dad got into it.

My brother Charlie showed up. Geri was there. It was kick ass, we had so much fun. We rode all through downtown, honking bike horns and waving and making a big spectacle of ourselves. I forget sometimes how much fun it is to spend time with people who think like me.

And there was this cute guy... he had a little girl with him, she was riding a bike on her own, she must have been about five or six. He seemed like a really nice dad, he watched out for her and joked with her. He wore a classy but weird top hat and ratty old tux that was perfect for the theme. We talked for a minute about bike trailers. I found myself wising I had never agreed to see Dexterous again.

And Dex? Who knows. I got home and checked my phone, which sure, I should have brought. But it hadn't had a charge when I needed to leave so I left it at home plugged in. There were four calls, every hour from 4:00 to 8:00. No text. One very slurry and drunken message at 5:00 saying something about please come meet him at The Red. He's drunk. Then nothing.

186

I tried to call back, but it went straight to voicemail. I wasn't too concerned at first, but then I started to wonder if he was OK. I decided eventually he was. But in the morning he texted, which is weird too. 6:00 in the morning, a text? He must have been worried. He said he'd gotten too drunk and passed out at "The Patersons". I didn't even know who they are. When I texted back, a question about what he was doing now, he never responded. For an entire day.

Ugh. Who needed that nonsense? I was too old, even then, for the drama. I just want to chill out with someone.

Retaliation

18 Months Ago

Here's the thing, I do have standards. Really.
But sometimes my standards are obscured by
sweet words and exuberance. And an ex-boyfriend
that just won't take a hint.

I met Andrew at the bar. Are you thinking,
what an awful mother? Or even, SHE is a teacher?
Please try to set your prejudice aside and
understand. Even mothers, even teachers, go out
on occasion. They even have fun and drink and

dance and -gasp!-have sex. Though we always feel guilty enough about it that we lose a large percentage of enjoyment, so don't worry. You aren't the only ones judging. We judge ourselves more.

But I am losing my point. Andrew. Andrew the waiter who I met at a bar. I went out with Sonara and Geri, attempting to stay away from Dex and our three-year "relationship." Geri really didn't want Sonara to go, I felt bad. It was one of those awkward nights where I was trying to make two friends who dislike each other comfortable. But then Andrew showed up and I kind of stopped worrying about Sonara talking about herself nonstop and Geri thinking she was irritating.

It started that Geri and I were supposed to go out to dinner, just the two of us. I had the boys all safely bundled off to my parents and her kids were with her husband and we were all set up for a great night of catching up. But right at the last minute Sonara called me with one of her frantic calls.

"Amanda!" Sonara said anxiously when I answered the phone.

"Sonara! How are you?" I asked her.

"Not great. I just found out Greg has been dating Trisha this whole time. This whole entire time! I was thinking we were so serious, that we might even get married, that any DAY now he would give me a ring. I even met his mom!"

I made some sympathetic noises, holding the phone between my shoulder and ear while I pulled hot rollers out of my hair. I was pleased my blonde hair looked bouncy and shiny..

"Amanda, I just can't be alone tonight. Can I come over? Emily is with my mom for the night," she gave a bitter laugh, "Ha! I thought Greg was going to take me out."

"Sure," I said, thinking Geri wouldn't mind too much.

But Geri had been annoyed. Which was weird because usually Geri accepted everyone.

"She takes advantage of you," Geri said to me when I called her and told her. "How often do you watch Emily?"

I frowned, thinking, "Well...maybe twice a week."

I could practically hear Geri roll her eyes, "See? TWICE a WEEK? Do you know how much you are saving her on childcare? Thousands of dollars a year. Not to mention, every time we go out you pay for her. I know how much you make teaching. You definitely cannot subsidize that woman anymore than I can. Why do you pay for her?"

I thought about it, I hadn't even know I was paying for Sonara. It always seemed like she ended up losing her wallet or forgetting it or...something."

So now, there I was at The Red with my two friends trying to make sure they got along. It was too loud to talk at this point so it didn't matter. But earlier when we were at dinner, at one of the fanciest places in town, our conversation was stilted.

"I love this place so much! LOVE it!" Sonara had gushed loudly, her voice filling the small restaurant. The other patrons had looked over at her, making Geri cringe in embarrassment.

Though Sonara was pretty and dressed in the most stylish clothes, she eventually lost her appeal because she never stopped to listen to anyone else.

Once the waiter arrived to take their order, Sonara had turned on the charm.

"Oh, THANK you," she said to the cute young guy as he brought out the menus, "I work in the industry and we hear such GOOD things about you here."

Geri looked at me flatly. Sonora often talked about "The Industry" as if she were an important wine maker or tourism guru instead of someone who bounced between tasting rooms and restaurants. I smiled. I just wanted my friends to get along.

The waiter, who was a tall dark-haired asian guy named Andrew, wasn't impressed with Sonara. Instead he kept his snapping dark eyes on me. When he took my drink order her smiled deeply at me, making me blush.

"I like a flavorful wine," I said to my friends when I ordered the L'Ecole.

Looking at me as if my friends weren't there he had murmured, "This wine is delicious, it lingers on your lips and warms your belly." He raised his eyebrows, looking deeply at me as he spoke.

I felt myself grow warm as he spoke in his smooth voice. Was he coming on to me? When he walked away, both Sonar and Geri giggled and Geri jabbed me with her finger.

"Someone has a crush on Amanda!" Geri said, smiling.

I blushed even more, looking down, "He's way too young for me!"

My friends laughed, making me glad they were together on something. I hoped maybe the night would go better for both of them after this.

And it had, a little. Sonara had continued talking a lot about herself, not listening, and even saying she didn't have money. But Geri was outspoken and simply stated that she needed to pay for herself or wash dishes - and amazingly Sonara had found money for her dinner. I statred to see what Geri was talking about.

Later, at The Red, we were dancing on the crowded dance floor when I felt a tap on my shoulder. I spun around, swaying my hips to the music, and was surprised to see the waiter, Andrew, standing behind me. I opened my mouth in surprise.

He smiled at me, holding out his hands and clasping mine. I let myself be guided by the young man, slightly embarrassed by how much younger he was than me. How old was he, anyway? 22? 23? He pulled my hands up, sliding his fingers up my bare arm. His eyes burned into me, taking in my form-fitting black jeans and halter top. He put his hand firmly on my waist, running his hand down my hip. He looked me deeply in the eye, making me dizzy. Who was this boy? I was surprised about how I was responding to him. I looked over my shoulder at Geri, who was (thankfully) dancing with Sonara, and smiled. Geri winked and gave me a little fist pump.

Later, Andrew invited me out to the deck and he offered me a cigarette. I laughed, accepting. I had smoked briefly in college, but I tried to avoid the addictive habit now. As I shared the cigarette with the young man we talked and laughed and I was surprised how smart he was.

"So," Andrew asked me, grinning, "What do you do when you aren't seducing young waiters?"

I laughed, "I teach high school Spanish."

He shook his head, "Wow, now I'm hot for teacher." He pulled me towards him, looking in my eyes. Then a movement over his shoulder caught my attention. I looked over the patio railing and was shocked to see Dex, standing on the sidewalk looking at me. He was standing with a group of his friends a few feet away. It looked like they had recently come out of a nearby restaurant. Dex was standing gape-mouthed, staring at me with a scowl on his face.

From: Dex
To: Amanda
11:30 pm

I know sometimes you have trouble doing what is right. I saw you at that bar, talking and dancing, smoking and drunk. I want to be with the good you, the nice Amanda. I wish you could be calm and loving.

From: Amanda
To: Dex
2:00 am

There was a little girl who had a little curl right in the middle of her forehead. And when she was good she was very, very good. But when she was bad she was HORRID.

It's Raining Men

It's Raining Men

Funny I would say that, considering I was
single and maybe, just maybe, a tiny bit lonely.
One of the worst parts about that time was how I
make a ton of fantastic food but my kids and
wouldn't even eat it. Charlie's dog liked it,
though. I remember all those years ago saying to
myself that I wish I just had someone to cook for.
This gives me hope, because my love now? He
loves my cooking. We eat dinner together now
nearly every night. And my boys love him too.

But at that time, a year and a half ago, I was trying so hard to forget Dex. Dex had really just been a cover up for the pain from Will, there were so many single men out there. Just none who stood out for me. Stupid ol' Dexterous still held sway over me, somehow, even though all we had never been serious for the majority of our "relationship." And sure, I still think about how he felt, etc....but after that incident with Anne trying to BEAT ME UP at a bar in Waitsburg, I was done with that whole icky crowd. I'll get to that in a minute. But at that time I needed to have more self-respect, dating around was never what I wanted.

Well, maybe.

I always tried to be classy. I think I probably came across as generally dignified, nice looking, my life in order. Even to this day I sometimes make money modeling and acting - ha ha! Who still models at my age? But local agencies call me and take my picture and the ads look pretty good. I'm in a few pictures advertising tourism here in our tourist town; and in some publications about health care, a couple of TV ads about banks and radio stations. Plus my teaching career was pretty good too. I generally enjoyed it, it was always challenging and interesting, even if education was losing funding and my pay kept getting cut.

But then there was my hidden life. The life where I would slink around the underbelly of our pretty little town, drinking beer, talking and laughing at bars, restaurants, even in scuzzy basements. When all the other good people, people with normal energy levels were home watching TV or sleeping, I was out living my second life. The life I never wanted anyone to know about. Sometimes the two lives would collide, even today at the grocery store when that totally freaky creep kept staring at me and then followed me around for a minute, trying to talk to me. Seriously? He's probably seen me singing karaoke at Mings. Yikes.

One Friday night, back after Dex and I really seemed like we were done, my mom I took the kids to opening night of our local baseball team. I got everybody bathed, read to, sang to and asleep. My mom was happy to stay over when I told her that I was going to Geri's for the tail end of her birthday party. I hopped on my bike, and careened across town carrying a six-pack of ESB. After visiting with Geri, Penny and a couple of other friends, I stopped at the Eagles to practice a couple of karaoke songs. Man, that place is gross. The bar was loaded with yike-o men, very drunk or special needs. Or both. I joined new acquaintances Carol, Marge, and Judy (who are, yes, as old as their names would suggest) and drank a beer and sang Midnight Special and Ain't Never. Marge sang Unchained Melody really well. While we waited our turns they asked me about myself, I explained a little about being single, divorced a few years, a little nervous of men.

Marge asked me how many men around town were following me around. At first I started to laugh, but these three women in their mid-70's were all looking at me, totally serious. I thought about it....and I answered that I guess three or four. They all nodded, yeah, men will follow you around. Don't ever tell 'em you've got money or they'll really start to harass you non-stop. Wow, that's bleak.

Did I have to tell Dexterous everything? He called me the next day, two days, I have to remind myself, after I saw him with trampy hairdresser Alison. I was already freaked out, I think my bipolar meds were off. Dex wanted to talk, he wanted to get together and try to "figure things out." I am so glad I said no! There are certain things I can't share with him, he's too black and white, too judgmental.

That evening I was walking with my kids, we were on our way to the park at the kids' request. It had been a wonderful day, church then a visit with my mom. I found out I had won a contest sponsored by our downtown, I'd hung out at my cousin Hank's house with our kids. I drank two beers then, feeling like a terrible mother, I got the kids packed up to go. As we were walking past a nearby church I glanced over and saw a young woman struggling to get a baby into a stroller while balancing a diaper bag and holding a puppy on a leash. Remembering that morning's sermon about the Good Samaritan, I walked over and offered to help her. She was grateful as I took the stroller and bag, removing my shoes as I carried the baby up the stairs so I wouldn't trip. Cody took her dog's leash and led the puppy up the stairs and Sam helped Winston follow along behind.

Once we got to the top, she directed me to a door at the end of the hall. This whole time we had been chatting about the puppy, how old her baby was, how she'd broken her leg and I hadn't asked her where she was going. But once I burst into the room carrying the stroller and the bag followed by Cody with the puppy, Sam, Winston, and the lady and her baby. I realized: we were at an AA meeting. It was sweltering hot outside, mid-afternoon on a Sunday, I'd just had two beers…and I was standing in the middle of a crowd of recovering alcoholics. I guess I felt guilty or just embarrassed, but somehow I couldn't just turn around and leave, I felt obligated to sit down on one of the folding chairs. The kids cheerfully joined a little group of kids playing with toys at the back as I looked around nervously. Before I knew it I was sucked into the meeting. People were very nice and honest and were taking turns sharing. When it came to my turn everyone just looked at me. I have not trouble speaking out in a group, I'm not shy, but I had no idea what I was supposed to talk about. I didn't want to give the whole Good Samaritan/afternoon beer/helping a stranger rundown, so I just stammered out my name and thank you for being helpful to people. Or something, my mind was swirling all over the place. It was nerve-wracking.

By the time I finally was able to get out of there I had learned a lot about some strangers and I was no longer very eager to go to the park. I went home, got dinner going, and answered a text from Dex (how are you?). I just said fine, making dinner. I never mentioned the AA meeting to him. I just can't tell him things like that. He'd get upset, I'm sure.

I wanted to tell him he's a fool. I would have loved him for the rest of my life if he had been the man to step up and love me back. Risked loving my children and me. I knew we would have made it work...but he was right, in a lot of ways we are wrong for each other - societally, in a modern way. 100 years ago, when what you watched on TV and who you voted for and what you did for fun didn't matter too much in mate selection, we would have been obvious. But the world has changed. I needed to realize we're just not going to work. I needed to go another direction, find that kind man who loves me and my family generously.

Dexterous would be happy with a cheap whore.

All day I had been upset by a boat dream where I was pushing stuff around a tilting boat, Dex was with some girl that looks just like him (same flannel shirt, same coloring). I knew what it meant, beyond any argument or doubt. I had to give him up, be done. I knew love was in my future and I would find it - but that if I waited too long I'd just be more hurt, hurt Dex, incite anger from his friends and family, not be available for love and have no resolution.

I needed ending and resolution and no more ambiguity.

Day 22: Getting a Little Worse Makes Me Better

Now: Day 22

I am proudly sober and healing. Not nearly so fragile…uh…until something comes up that stresses me out. Thankfully today's freakout wasn't witnessed by anyone.

Yeah I'll make a scene. For no reason. I will sit on the edge of my bed, phone in my lap, hyperventilating because some doctor's office didn't bill my insurance and I'm convinced I can't handle any of this anymore. The paperwork, the piles of endless papers that arrive at my house and require I do something, anything, with them. And I do, for years and years and years I have meticulously paid every bill, filed every file, thrown out every piece of garbage. And I have this perfect credit and these labeled files and all my shit should be taken care of.

But it doesn't stop and I'm starting to wonder if I'm going to be able to continue doing this for the rest of my life. All of this. Paying the mortgage, the electric bill, the gas. Taking my car in for maintenance. Taking kids to the doctor and then getting them the medicine or whatever. Then trying to figure out if the fucking insurance paid the bill. Or not. Or if they were billed. And through all of it wading through about fifty different login and passwords and please call our customer service line during office hours so you can sit on hold listening to goddamn Vivaldi while the one person we hired to man the phones farts around and might or might not get back to you.

Work? Work? When would a person have time to work with all the phone purgatory they have to sit through. I just feel like I've reached my threshold for being able to tolerate the endless systems we have to deal with every day. And I wonder if I'm actually even here. Am I even alive? Am I visible? I must be, but with the amount of times lately people forget to send me information or forget to bill my insurance, or forget to email me the start time of my new class schedule….I'm starting to wonder if I didn't die a few months ago and no one bothered to tell me.

Big gaping holes in my memory, people saying things are happening and I don't have any inkling of them happening. Or people saying things didn't happen and I know they did. Phone calls going in circles. Please wait. Please hole. Vivaldi. I sent that. They called you. We billed them. You owe us. This happened, it is in your chart. It might not have been two days ago, but it's in your chart now. It happened.

Why does this bother me so much? It's just insurance. It's only $450, my entire month's food budget, going to pay for the psychiatrist I need to see to deal with the stress from my job, my life. The stress from not having enough money. The stress from sitting on hold for forty minutes to talk about how insurance won't pay for what they're supposed to pay. So then we won't have money for food. But psychiatry soothes me into thinking my mental illness is getting fixed. Ha ha. Every bit of regulated brain wave is now haywire.

I think the real solution might be to just go away, start walking toward whatever dirt hut I can find. Live with real problems. No paper or internet WiFi. No phone hell. No doctors or billing or Department of Social Services. Just me and some horseflies and leeches, just wallowing around dealing with real problems. Genuine stuff that I can see and touch and understand. No password errors or trying to recall usernames. No cloud or charge or inbox. None of it. Just trying to find shelter and food and clean water.

Would I be wringing my hands, panicking, tears streaming down my face if I had to outrun a tiger? Would I be screaming at soft-spoken ladies over a telephone about ID cards and claims if my neighbors had cholera? How about if I had to get up in 2 hours, when the sun comes up, to harvest our crops with everyone else - would I be frantically going through metal drawers full of ten-year-old paper, analyzing each number for potential payment? Probably not. I might not be any happier, but it wouldn't matter if I was happy. I probably wouldn't also be a ridiculous pile of jittery tears and snot and shallow breathing, convinced I'm going to lie down in some gutter and die because of some messed up insurance card.

Thankfully the phone hell robots don't know me and no real human being got to witness my melt down. Am I going to start my period? Oh, yes, I am going to start my period…go meditate Amanda. Go take a walk outside. Drink some water, girl, get yourself under control. Breathe.

Road Trip from Hell

Two(ish) Years Ago: Late Summer

And freaking out at stuff on the phone that upsets me, it can't help but remind me of other failed relationships. Was I drawing this all toward myself? Was it me? First there was Carlisle moving away and never really talking to me again. Then Will. Then all the crap with Dex that never seemed to end - for years! But equally painful was when my relationship exploded with my friend Sonara.

Sonara is really sweet and pretty and seems great, in fact I considered her a close friend. I didn't heed the warnings of my friends and family when they told me it was strange how I would babysit her daughter twice and three times a week, how I fed them the same amount of time, sometimes dinner and breakfast since Sonara would eat before leaving her daughter for the night then eat again upon picking her up in the morning. I also didn't heed my inner voice when Sonar awould always promise to do things for me ("Come over for dinner!" "Let me fix that sweater, I'll bring it back I promise!" "I'll pay next time!") but then never follow through.

I was too busy having fun, laughing and enjoying a friend who was as interested in getting dressed up and dancing and telling fun stories as I am. I liked listening to her never-ending accounts of unrequited love and her post-midnight adventures. She was fun and interesting and I didn't pay much attention to how she might be for day-to-day life.

So when she talked me into driving her across the state to pick up her daughter from her dads a more than 400 mile journey, I had my misgivings, but she was so smooth and so promising and so upbeat about the whole trip that I pushed any doubts out of my mind. My kids would be out of town with their dad for the weekend and a fun road trip sounded more pleasant than three days home alone.

But the warnings of my mom ("She's a shyster!") and Geri ("Make sure she pays for herself") rang around my head louder and louder the further we got from home. I won't go into it other than after ten hours in the car with her I was pretty anxious for the trip to be over. She wouldn't use a map, declaring she knew the route like the 'back of her hand', refusing to accept when we were hopelessly lost. Yelling at me when we couldn't reach our destination because we had gotten lost and had to sleep in my car. Very reluctantly paying when it was her turn to buy gas, arguing about turns. Not ordering then eating my food, calling me selfish when I didn't pay for her. Etc, etc. Not fun. But I quietly endured, mildly put out. I was still determined to have fun.

Once we arrived I discovered she had another agenda. A guy. Of course there would be a guy. I was happy for her - and happy to have some space when she disappeared with him for the day. I was slightly surprised when she never introduced me, but I realized later it was a hook up, he has a girlfriend. She, though, seemed surprised when he wouldn't return her numerous texts and phone calls afterwards. I didn't say much other than to advise her to let him be, my experience with men is the harder you push the more they run. And, hey, he has a girlfriend. But push she did and run HE did. True to form, she got upset. But unlike our past experiences when we would drink some wine, lament her woes, eat my food, and she would go home...this time we had to travel six hours back home. 700 miles in the car with a woman scorned? Not a good scene. Especially since, as she pointed out repeatedly, I am selfish and didn't give her the level of sympathy she felt I should give. I had the gall to smile over a kind text from Andrew. I didn't buy her lunch. I sprayed a water bottle in the car and it made noise. My book on tape was too loud.

When we picked up her daughter to drive her home she transferred her irritation to her daughter - yelling at her for making even the slightest noise, or asking any questions, or needing a drink. But I wasn't completely off the hook. I was such a bitch I told her I didn't want to sleep sitting up on the side of the road, I'd prefer to stop at a camp ground. This bizarre disagreement set her off on a thirty-minute tirade against me, leaving me shaking and fighting back tears as she spoke loudly and angrily about how selfish, condescending, immature, and annoying I am. When she said we should just not speak any more I said, "YES! Let's not speak any more." But she really, really wanted to argue. She attempted to get me to speak, but I just shook my head and said no, I won't do this.

I would have let her out, been done with the situation, but we were four hours from home and her nine-year-old daughter already had to endure her mother. Being stuck on the side of the road at 11:00 at night would be inhumane, so I silently endured her wrath. It was terrible. I'm not proud to say I was not able to stand up for myself very well. The situation reminded me of life with my ex-husband, especially my fear and mamby-pamby ineptitude. I couldn't bear to go down to her level, I just couldn't yell or insult her. It was a nightmare. We drove mainly in silence all night, she only yelled a couple more times, particularly when I asked her if she wanted to pull over and camp at midnight. Absolutely not. She drove the last three hours, pulling into her driveway at two in the morning. I would have driven away then, disgusted, but still pretty intact, if it weren't for her last hurrah.

Blocking my exit from her driveway, she yelled at me yet again. Recounting the same insults from before. I am selfish. I don't care about anyone but myself. I talk too much. No one likes me. I am condescending. On and on, repeating and repeating as I sat mute, taking her abuse. Numb and stunned. She finally stopped when I spoke up. I yelled out for her to stop insulting me. I forcefully said I see why people cut her out of their lives, why her family won't speak to her. With one final scream at me to "GROW UP!!! You need to adjust your meds!" she stormed off.

Whoa. Note to self: choose road-trip companions very wisely.

Done

Day 22

Spring is beginning to arrive. I have always felt hopeful when the days start to get a little longer, birds start to twitter in the morning and that little thrill of life awakening comes into my blood. After this winter I needed something to wake me up. I didn't bounce back from Sonara freaking out on me the summer before last, especially so soon after Anne. I'll get to Anne later. But what happened at that time? Am I really so wrath-inspiring? After Sonara I spent days, no weeks, wallowing in my head wondering if I somehow deserved to have people attack me. I had to come to the conclusion that of course I did. Otherwise it wouldn't have happened. Just like with my ex-husband, I selected him and chose to spend time with him. I didn't leave despite the warnings. So even though I didn't deserve to be yelled at or injured...I still found myself in that predicament because I did not walk away. I ignored the warning signs.

And I had many chances to learn. Dex and his by unkind friends. Again, I saw the warnings. I saw that Dex wouldn't defend me, that his friend (Married-But-Looking) Mike's wife, Anne, was her own special brand of crazy. And did I refuse to spend time with her? Did I tell Dex, "It's them or me?" Oh no, I would never do that. I wouldn't want to be demanding or impolite, right? So I just passively sat there, waiting for her to lash out at me. And, you know, her verbal attack was not really that big. Another type of woman, say Erica or Maria or Geri, would have just stood up for herself. Would have just told mean Anne to shut her jealous trap. But me, oh no...I just cried, ran, acted guilty and afraid. No wonder she freaked out. I'm weak.

Then Sonara. Over. The. Top. That was crazy and I just sat there and took it. Come to think of it so did Emily, poor kid. We just sat there mute while Sonara went nuts on us. It wasn't until I finally yelled at her to stop insulting me that she finally shut up.

I've been thinking about this for awhile. All those years married to a scary man taught me to shut up and follow directions without complaint, right? And this didn't just go away, even though I tried to choose better with Dex and I went to counseling. I still managed to find assholes to mistreat me. I think this lesson was going to keep coming and coming until I finally got enough of a backbone to stand up for myself without having to cry or run.

So my boys have seen this in me a little bit. Not much, mind you, I shield my kids nightly from all the nonsense running around my head. They met Dex a handful of times, and always just as a friendly visitor. They never met Andrew, though I only went out with him for a few weeks, so why would they have? Their dad may have freaked out, but they never saw that either. I know life has dumped on us a bit, but I have protected them fiercely and they are happy, well-adjusted, calm boys who are enjoying life. But they also see that I struggle with standing up for myself. Because it's not just their dad. It's not just drunk ladies at bars or narcissists mooching rides across the state. It's the lady cutting in front of me in line at the grocery store. It's the PTA mom telling me I'm sitting in her seat at the Christmas program. It's the guy at the bank rudely telling me to 'contain my children' when they were being perfectly polite. And me just taking it. Turning the other cheek. But Cody recently asked me why I don't stand up for myself and I realize he is right. It's one thing to not fight back. It's another to allow others to stomp all over me.

At work, a few weeks into the school year, this lady I work with - Christine - started to bulldoze me. She often tromps all over people, she's kind of stocky and talks really loud and hopes to be a principal someday. She has her good traits - she has parties and invites the whole staff. She always says hi to people. She volunteers for all the crap no one wants to do. But she also takes over even when the project might belong to someone else. She doesn't listen very well. And she tells other people what to do even when she has no right to.

That's what happened, she decided to tell me I needed to do something. The details don't matter much other than that we are on the same committee and both she or I should have contacted a couple of other teachers. Since that OR is in there neither of us contacted the other teachers so information was not relayed. She approached me in the staff room after the meeting and said in an aggressive voice, "Why did you not tell Sean and Chuck about the change to the teaching materials?"

I got flustered, as I always do when confronted, and I stammered something about not realizing I needed to talk to them.

She spoke even more loudly and angrily, "Well, you DROPPED the BALL! You need to communicate with the entire upstairs hallway!"

Then she spun off and marched away, leaving me near tears. Again feeling like I had been sucker-punched and I wasn't sure what I had done to deserve it.

But just at that moment my best friend Maria came into the staff room. Seeing my stricken face she asked what was wrong.

"It's Christine…she just reprimanded me." I said softly, trying not to cry.

Maria looked confused, "How could she reprimand you? She teaches reading. You teach Spanish. She is your colleague. She can't reprimand you."

But then Maria, how I love women like Maria, surprised me. She didn't commiserate with me and start talking about what a mean woman Christine is. Nope, instead she said, "Just send her an email. Tell her you don't like how she talked to you."

And that was it. Discussion closed. No wonder Maria has no drama. That's exactly what she would do, too. I asked her for a little guidance on what to say and then I ran upstairs and drafted an email. But just before hitting send I decided I needed to go one step further. I wasn't going to just hide behind my computer and stand up for myself. No! I needed to tell Christine in person. So I read the email to myself, getting my words just right, then I hopped up and walked down to the lunch room where I hoped to find Christine. Providence intervened. She was standing right in front of me when I rounded the corner.

"Christine," I called, "I need to talk to you."

She swung her arms, all cool and disinterested. Still mad at me for not doing a job she could have done herself.

I looked her right in the eye, took a deep breath, and said, "I don't appreciate you reprimanding me."

She immediately cut me off, "You didn't do your job!"

I got mad. She hadn't done her job either and it was an honest mistake on both of our part. Even though my heart was beginning to pound in my ears I stepped toward her. I was delighted to realize I towered over her in my platform heels by at least six inches.

I looked down at her and said in a low, firm voice, "Christine, you are not my boss. It is not your place to reprimand me. Please do not do it again."

Her eyes widened as she looked up at me. "OK," she said softly, "I won't"

"Thank you," I said. Then I turned and walked off.

The funny thing is, after that Christine treated me with a lot more respect. And the even funnier thing was that when I was recounting the story that night to Charlie and the boys at dinner, Cody surprised me by smiling at the end of the story and adding:

"Mom, you were great. But you shouldn't have said please."

Charlie and I looked at each other and smiled.

"Really?" I asked my oldest. "Was please too polite?"

He nodded, his sweet face earnest, "Way too polite. You should have said something to her a long time ago. She needs to learn to treat people better."

I laughed, "I think she will."

"Good job, Mom," he added.

I beamed. I felt pretty good about it myself.

I got a chance to put my newfound mojo to use just a few days later.

Erica needed us. The moment I heard Jim Jackson had died I had called Erica and left a message, telling her to call when she needed someone to talk to. I was surprised yet not surprised when I got a text from Erica saying she was in town. Who could blame her? Los Angeles is probably a cool place to be when things are going well…but when things are falling apart? Maybe not. So Geri, Penny, and I planned a girls night for the first night Erica would be in town. It was sad to see her so upset, we had all enjoyed Jim but Erica really knew him well. He had always been this really cool guy: funny, smiling, calm, a good listener. It was hard to believe he was gone. But one look at Erica's swollen eyes and it drove the loss home. Jim Jackson was gone.

I personally don't have any experience with heroine or any other drugs other than the occasional joint passed around at parties or late at night after the kids are asleep. But somehow the wild party life had led Jim to a heroine addiction. More surprising, Penny admitted that her ex-husband Ricky also had a heroine addiction. Wow. It's hard to realize that all people have problems. I have been so caught up in my own drama in the past few years that I haven't even noticed that other people around me have a lot going on too. Divorce, little children, not enough money, trying to date…these are distracting. But at least no one around me has a terrible addiction. I felt bad for not paying better attention to my friends.

We were having a really great night, just catching up and visiting, when Penny finally asked me about Carlisle. I blushed immediately, surprising myself. I thought he and I were through years ago, but just the mention of his name brought all our good times flooding back.

My friends laughed at my obvious discomfort at the mention of Carlisle.

"Wow, someone seems to have some feelings going on," Geri said, smiling.

I shook my head, "No, that is ancient history."

Erica raised her eyebrows, "He's single, you know. He hasn't dated anyone in quite awhile. Who knows…maybe you two will end up seeing each other around sometime."

I raised my eyebrows back at her, "What about Simone?"

Erica laughed, "That wasn't real! Ask him when you see him."

I shook my head, "See him? Well…I can imagine you might arrange something!"

Everyone laughed, Erica had been known to try to arrange "accidental" meetings between people before. She liked to see herself as a matchmaker.

A couple nights later we all went out on the town. I didn't see Carlisle, which was probably a good thing considering I was still trying to figure out how to get over Dex. But I did have a revelation:

My brother Charlie was playing at a popular local night spot with a group of friends. He doesn't like when I say 'with his band' because he thinks he's too old to be trying to make it as a musician. So whenever my parents or I talk about his music hobby we have to carefully word it as if he and his friends just get together and play music. I guess that IS what having a band is, right? We can't all be like Erica and have ten million people buy our album and come to our concerts.

So Charlie and the guys were just getting started, playing a fun and lively song Charlie had written, when I glanced over my shoulder. I was sitting with my mom at a table toward the front of the stage, enjoying the warm bar lit mainly by candles. I felt pretty content, I hadn't seen Dex in a few weeks and, more importantly, I didn't want to. I'm not sure what caused me to turn around but I think it was the sound of forced laughter. I looked without really thinking about it and was surprised to see Sonara and even more surprised to see she was sitting with…Dex. Sonara was flipping her hair all around, her hand resting on his arm, laughing her head off about something he had just said.

My first impulse was to run. I couldn't believe the gall of this woman who had been, until our road trip a good friend. She was out on a date with my ex-boyfriend? And not some long-ago ex-boyfriend, either. I felt my neck flush hot and my heart started to pound.

"What is it?" my mom whisper-shouted toward my ear, but she didn't wait for a response. Instead she followed my gaze and saw Sonara and Dex laughing together towards the back of the room. Sonara was still flipping her hair around, tugging at top, which was a strapless tube top.

My mom looked back at me with an expression that clearly said, "Are you kidding me?" I nodded and shrugged. It was too loud to really be able to talk, but I was glad my mom was on my side.

Just at that minute Erica walked up to my table. She looked a lot better than she had the last time we had gotten together, more cheerful and without puffy eyes. In fact, her eyes were all sparkly and she wore a great big grin. She kept looking over at Charlie and then smiling even bigger. I looked at my brother, on stage, and saw that he was smiling really big too. What was going on? Had these two finally figured it out? For a brief second I forgot about my ex-friend and ex-boyfriend clearly on a date just behind me. Charlie had liked Erica since he was a kid, that would be great if they finally got together!

As I looked at her, so happy, and him, doing what he loves and also very happy, I realized Dex would never make me happy like that. Sonara could have him. They could have each other. Dex would never just accept me the way Charlie had always accepted Erica. I would never be able to just look at Dex and feel good about us, he was wrong for me. And without even thinking about it further I stood up. My mom and Erica both looked up at me in surprise, wondering where I was going. It was still too loud to be able to explain anything so I just tilted my head toward Dex and Sonara, still laughing their heads off. They both immediately understood and looked surprised because I'm not usually one to stand up for myself. My mom smiled and nodded slightly, she was proud of me that I was doing something about Dex and Sonara.

I didn't really have a plan, but I knew I needed to do something. Pushing my shoulders back I stood straight and tall and, I hoped, beautiful. I plastered a big cheery smile on my face and walked over to Sonara and Dex. They still hadn't see me. Dex was yelling over my brother and his band, telling her all about his wood stove (seriously? Does the man ever talk about anything else??). I approached their table and stood there until they both looked up. Not letting my smile fall at all, despite the immediate scowl Sonara flashed or the look of shocked guilt covering Dex's face.

I waved my hand cheerfully and yelled over the music, "Hey guys! Looks like you're having a good night!"

Dex stood up, his face frozen in shame, "Amanda, I - "

I smiled even more broadly and called out, "Have fun!" I turned away, starting out for my own table again. My mom and Erica were both watching me, wide-eyed.

By the time I slid back into my seat (my mom and Erica giving me nearly imperceptible looks of 'good job!') Dex and Sonara were gathering their things together and slinking out the back door. Hey, they could feel guilty about this if they wanted to. I just felt free!

After that I could sit back and enjoy the rest of the show. I even got to witness Charlie sneak a kiss from Erica when he was done playing. I had a good feeling about those two!

Day 23

Day 23

I love how, the first day I started writing this, from the Emergency Room, I titled it 30 Days to Overcoming a.....big long description of what I felt like I was dealing with. And now here it is Day 23 and I feel better, yes, but that Day 30 is looming big and scary. Like, what if in a week I am still fucked up? What if I still have meltdowns and cry? Now I'm sober, I'm not on any medication - but I'm not a stable person, not really. I'm not like those content people out there blissfully walking around without crazy ruminations or self-loathing thoughts. Although, I guess I am a bit better. I can at least recognize when things are getting hectic. I can at least use some of my techniques for calming down - meditation, a walk, a drink of water. Deal with the old junk.

Leaving a Bad Situation

Even though I knew Dex was wrong for me, I always eventually gave in and saw him again. I wish I hadn't, but when he kept calling and telling me how much he likes me…well, I'm just a week fool. That summer before last, just a couple of weeks before the terrible road trip with Sonara, we went out to the Salmon Feed, out in Waitsburg. We went with Dex's friends, Craig, Richelle, and also Married-But-Looking and his wife, Anne. It wasn't really my scene but I made the most of it, I wore my cowboy boots and a Carhart jacket and at least appeared to fit in. But everybody had the same dumb redneck conversations. Seriously, what is is about uneducated people? Can't they see how petty and mean they are when they talk about how much they hate other people? I promise, the intelligent, liberal-minded, free-thinking people I prefer to spend time with almost NEVER say anything about people who are different from us. What is there to say? Really? We can only shake our heads at people who refuse to recycle or who think they can make someone's sexual preferences illegal. Why waste time having a conversation about ideas that are so ignorant?

But these same ignorant people, on the other hand, continuously bash the other side. It is so hateful and tiresome to listen to Dex's friends make fun of liberals, gays, anyone who isn't white, and "weirdos." Or maybe, just maybe, I am being as ignorant as they are in assuming that all people like them do the same thing. Maybe these assholes only did this in front of me. Hmmm.....

But to get to the point. Anne, remember Anne? Married-But-Looking's unfriendly wife? She tried to beat me up that last night I went out with Dex. Yes, that's right. Beat. Me. Up. It happened, a grown woman, a woman who has two children and a husband and goes to a nice job at a bank every morning drank too much and shoved me and then held her fist up and screamed at me. But I'm getting ahead of myself.

After the Salmon Feed we went to the Anchor Bar down the street from the Waitsburg Grange Hall. My cousin Hank and his wife Lori were there. Everyone always loves Hank, so he and Lori joined us. I just wasn't into it. I was still pretty pissed about Dex not showing up and the not calling and then the passing out at The Petersons house shit with no explanation. And really, I was just about done. Done. So I wasn't really sitting with Dex and MBL and Anne and Hank and Lori and Richelle and Craig. Instead I was at the bar, talking to a girl I had gone to school with. And, I'll admit it, trying to find someone to smoke some pot with. Or at least a cigarette.

Finally Dex got a clue that I was not into it and he asked if I wanted to go home. I said yes I did and we got our coats on. MBL had come up to the bar too, I guess to order a beer. I said good-bye to MBL, giving him a small hug. A side-arm hug.

Chaste. This guy is not interesting to me and never has been. But Anne jumped up and stumbled over and, as I was stepping back from MBL saying "See ya later," Anne shoved me with both hands. She was furious.

What did I do after that? I had to wonder if I was sending off some signal that I deserve to be screamed at or pushed down? Or did I somehow seek out people who are violent because I secretly want to be abused still? Whatever it is, I really do not want it to happen and I just shook my head at Anne and held up my hands.

"Are you OK?" I asked her, trying to stay calm.

Both MBL and Dex were holding her, she was practically frothing at the mouth as she tried to swing at me. She screamed at me, "Don't hug my husband! Stay the fuck away from him!"

My heart was beating so hard I couldn't even speak. I didn't wait for anybody, the fight or flight instinct hit and I FLEW! I ran out the door without my purse and I didn't stop running until I had reached the highway. Thoughts of Sonara, screaming at me. Will with the knife over his head. The bat. The TV. I fell to the ground, in the dark, and just sobbed. Hank and Lori pulled up beside me pretty quickly after that. They had my purse and got me to ride home with them. Dex wanted me to go with him, but I really didn't want to talk to him. Especially when the first text he sent me asked only what I had done to make Anne so mad. What I had done? I don't think I did anything except be attractive and speak to her philandering husband.

Seriously, was it because of local modeling and being on stupid commercials, is this why women like Anne hate me? They are magazine and TV ads! It's not like I'm some superstar, I stand in front of a damn camera and hold up shopping bags or pretend to help a sick patient. Man, I wonder what truly talented and successful actresses and models and rock stars like Erica do. Are they totally lonely? Do they just have to hang out with other people like them? No, most women aren't scary insecure like Sonara or Anne, most don't care at all. They see my looks as temporary or unimportant just like I do. It's only really unstable people who get upset about a pretty or successful rival.

But Dex, really? What did I do to make Anne so mad? So when he texted, what did I do? I didn't even respond. Never. After all this time he probably still assumes I did something horrible and some girl shoving me and holding her fist up at me was justified. Just like the time he told his friend Craig I wasn't technically an abused wife because "she was never punched in the face."

Why did I waste my time? I'm glad I got away and stayed away.

More fun morsels

The Fall Before Last Fall

After that night at the Salmon Feed, I just -
boom - didn't want to be around Dex anymore. I
felt like I was cured!

Then it was fall, one of those fall days so lovely
it's easy to not notice because it seems life should
just BE this way. You know, like you don't notice
how nice it is to have good parents or a
comfortable home or a loving friend. That day was
bright and blue and the yellow leaves on all the

trees kept catching my eye. Soccer, playing with my kids, a meaningful conversation with my Aunt Gloria. I hadn't seen Dex in six weeks. I just didn't want to deal with his inability to commit.

Then I ran into him at the grocery store. Maybe the only time I've ever run into him and actually had it be a genuine accident instead of a contrived "accident." And sure, he was cute. And strong. And really funny. But…come on, who needed his nonsense? Who needed a man who promises the world and then can't commit? Who needed a man who is constantly scrutinizing me, deciding if I might be worth it? Who tried to make me change the most fundamental parts of myself? Not me. I was done.

So even though he stood and talked to me in the produce aisle for awhile, then again near the fish, I just wasn't interested. Was it because he hardly said anything to my boys, other than to tell them to be careful not to knock the apple display over? Come on! Like I'm not watching them. Now that I think about it, he was always like that with my kids, never really connecting to them, just telling them what to do or being nervous about them. Not to mention, why does he get to be this awesome Christian all the time, while considering me some not-quite-good-enough Christian? Just because I go to a quiet church where people don't wave their hands around and yell out 'Praise Jesus' all loud does not make me any less of a Christian. Ugh. Sometimes I feel like he's just trying to SHOW everyone how religious he is, instead of just simply BEING religious. Who needs it?

After I saw him, the first time since horrible Anne freaked out at that bar, I called him. I don't know why, I guess I was thinking we could talk about it, make moving on easier. But he didn't answer. And he never even called back, he just sent a stupid email. By that point I was so sick of having a guy email me instead of talk to me. I was so tired of having a relationship that was going no where. I detested his circular logic. So I let him go! My response to his stupid, meaningless, maybe-this-will-work, maybe-it-won't email was just a final, definitive, SLICE. Finally. Here's this little email exchange: (Note: unedited. He always had spelling errors)

_____

From: dexterousdoesit@engineeringfirm.com

To: TeacherAmanda@hometownmail.com
Subject: Hello
November 16 at 6:14 PM

Good morning Amanda,

I couldn't return your call. I was with the guys.

   I awoke sad early this morning thinking about
you and the kids, they need all of your love.
furthermore my interaction with you all may not
have had a positive impact on your lives. The
number one thing in all of this is God and a close
second are the kids and stability for you and
ultimately them. I am so sorry for not being able to
provide that and make everything ok. It is not an
easy thing to take on. As a man I feel as if it is my
duty and I could not. I may have made things
worse for you all maybe life would have been
more stable without me in it. One will never know
for sure? Perhaps, when we met, had God not put
us together our lives would be in ruin from other
choices? Who knows what would have been had
we not found each other in a time where we were
both venerable and perhaps a bit careless. Perhaps
Gods plan is right on track? Looking forward the

right path has been found to take time and heal. I know God has happiness and good things for store for you if you trust in his promises.

I wrote you this in the am and have not had a chance to send it until now. One of those days even lunch hour had a meeting.

Work is picking up a bit. Lots of miracles expected by sales, cut work force and increase output. Doesn't always work.

I will talk to you later.

Keep smiling

Dex

_____

From: TeacherAmanda@hometownmail.com
To: dexterousdoesit@engineeringfirm.com
Subject: Hello?
November 16 at 7:30 AM

Dexterous:

Venerable? Yep. That's why we had sex after 10 days and then spent the next three years almost committing and not being able to love (you) and being full of self-loathing and running away (me). Mmmm hmmmm.... venerable.

Or did you mean vulnerable? Like I really needed a good, strong man to protect, love, respect, cherish, and BE THERE for my tiny boys and me? A man who sticks to his word, you know - the kind of man who when he says "I want to have children, I want to meet your kids, I want to make my house a home, I need someone to complete me...." He actually MEANS it? Is that what you mean by vulnerable? A single mom who is hiding from an abusive ex-husband is a tad bit vulnerable. I don't know, maybe not as vulnerable as a cuckolded husband. Hard to compare.

But I'm really glad God put us together to keep you from ruin. I, on the other hand, am much worse off. I now trust men even less than I did three years ago - because now I know that even men who say they are very honest are still deceitful and manipulative. A man who knows what his duty is but who, even though he can't fulfill it, continues to string a vulnerable single mom along. Just to make sure she doesn't move on and possible try to find a man who can fulfill the extremely difficult duty of stepping up to the plate.

But cliches are true. And my lack of boundaries caused "why buy the cow when the milk is free" to be an absolute reality. So I can now continue on to detest myself and my venerability that led me to trust foolishly once again. Because yes, I am venerable. I am a good person. Are you? Sorry, that's mean. I'm mad. Of course you're a good person. Being unable to commit just because I needed you to doesn't make you evil. I realize this. However, not letting me go when you knew you couldn't follow through with the mature action was .... selfish. Maybe cowardly.

I called you yesterday because I missed you. I needed you. I ached for love and trust and a good man. And I know I have played a huge role in this whole debacle - I haven't ever just walked away like I should have. I guess I've strung you along, too - because I'm so full of hope that you'll change. That you'll be the man I imagine you are capable of being. But I am not being loving toward myself of my kids by allowing this to continue. A man who goes out drinking 2, 3 times a week is not ready for the kind of care and maturity I need.

So I read this email from you last night. I hear you still not committing. Still not loving me or my kids. Still only concerned with your own self....and I am done. My heart hurts - but not as bad as when I saw that picture of you ogling Sonara's boobs right before you called her the moment I walked away. Or knowing you went hunting with Alison. Or when you brought Sonara to hear my brother play music. Or all the times you responded to my declarations of love with "I LIKE you." Yeah. My heart doesn't hurt like that now. It just hurts that I have wasted so much time on you And that you have let me go to find that love that will do right by me, appreciate me and my beautiful family.

So yeah. This is the venerable choice. The venerable action.

Have a good life Dex. I hope you heal without hurting anyone else.

Me

From: dexterousdoesit@medicalclinic.com
To: TeacherAmanda@hometownmail.com
Subject: Hello?

November 16 at 9:14 AM

Wow that's mean.

If you need to talk call.
I have more to say but have a conference call
now.

DDD

_____

Day 24

Day 24

After all these years, thinking about Dex and the stupid pain he caused....I feel such relief and freedom that I am over him. I am no longer mad at him, it just wasn't a relationship that was going to work. Will? That may still take some time. Dex, not being able to commit, not understanding me? That was nothing compared to how my ex-husband treated me. I wonder if all that time I spent fretting about Dex was really just a way to bury the real pain, like pharmaceuticals and alcohol after Dex and I broke up. That true genuine pain that isn't even really worth writing about - the pain of getting married young, to a man I love love loved. A man I had tons of friends with and enjoyed having fun with. A man who was also a teacher and who shared my beliefs and hopes. A man I bought a beautiful house with and had beautiful children with. A man who I was married to for ten years who, on occasion, lost his shit and treated me like garbage. A man I eventually worried would kill me in a fit of temper…a man who, to this day, has access to my babies and I am terrified of what could happen.

Of course I look for distraction.

Day of The Dead

Describing domestic violence is not something
I want to do, but there are times when I know I
need to get out there and do it. When I was first on
the run from my volatile and violent ex-husband I
searched desperately for information or solace
about domestic abuse, I went to the library, online,
and to the YWCA looking for women with a story
similar to mine. I found a lot of women who had
struggled and suffered horrible indignity at the
hands of not just their husbands and boyfriends but
often their parents and others around them too.
One girl told me she had been locked in a cage and

burned by an evil man, for over a year. Another girl told of having her hair pulled and being thrown down the stairs. As I listened to women from all walks of life, I came to a realization: every single story is different. But there is one similarity: the sense of accomplishment we feel when we get ourselves together well enough to walk away.

For me, I wouldn't consider my situation to be all too extreme, though I don't think it is fair to downplay it simply because it wasn't bloody. I was married to a man who would fly into unpredictable rages, who called me "F-ing B" more than my name, who did not acknowledge me when I spoke, and who threatened me with a knife and a baseball bat. It happened infrequently enough that I simply had little respect for him and wished he would go away, but not often enough that I was aware of how scary a situation I was actually in.

It wasn't until our children were born, though, that his temper really got the best of him. Let's see.....should I really write this? My kids will read this someday. I could just gloss it over, make it a glib little, "Oh, he wasn't that bad!" in the fake falsetto so many of us use, couldn't I? But I myself hate reading and listening to lies and I can spot them a mile away. My children love their dad and want him to be a good person. Now, years after I left him, he has turned himself around. There were a couple of years after everything fell apart when Will could have just disappeared from our lives forever, but I didn't let it happen. And, no, this is not because I am weak. This is because I myself had a good relationship with my dad and I know how important this is. I trusted that Will would eventually get the help he needed and get himself together well enough to at least know our children, even if he allowed his stupid temper to destroy all of our lives for awhile. Well, those lives forever, we had to begin new lives. But this little disclaimer can act as a bookend for what will follow, so if anyone reading this who knows me tries to judge my kids or me for allowing him to still be in our lives, understand that regardless of his flaws, he will always be my kids' dad.

The day our lives ended was not the first fight. I had left Will briefly the Valentines Day before. When I returned to him my family was disappointed in me. But I would always start to trust him again, I would believe him when he told me it would never happen again. This time Will was teaching at a nearby elementary school and was planning on taking the following week off to begin his three month leave to care for our infant son, Winston, our three-year-old son, Cody, and two year old son, Sam. I was set to go back to work in just a couple of days. Winston was a tiny baby, his birth gone perfectly, he had ended up back in the hospital at two weeks old because of a urinary tract infection. It was awful. That evening we had gone to a birthday party for my cousin Hank. Even though he had been napping for three hours, Winston wouldn't wake up. Everyone around me was partying and having fun and my tiny infant wouldn't eat or stir and no one really paid any attention. All of my family members just dismissed my concern as me being over-protective. My mom, who would have instantly have known better, was visiting a friend out of town, and everyone else was preoccupied with talking and festivities. I finally called the doctor who told me to take the baby immediately to the emergency room. Once I arrived, I realized how grave the situation was because the doctors and nurses all started to freak out. I had been pretty nervous before arriving, thinking my baby was sick. But once I got there and saw the medical personnel running franticly and circling my baby I realized they thought he might die. When no one could get an IV into his limp arm they told me to go wait in the hall. I calmly said, no, I will stay in the room with my son. Thank God for Dr. Wren who somehow managed to get an IV into the top of Winston head. As soon as he did my baby went from limp and white to pink and alive. I am so grateful.

We spent the next three weeks in the hospital, I spent nights at home but most of the day with Winston. Will's mom, Pam, came and helped Will with Sam and Cody. Our family really struggled at this time. When Winston finally was able to leave, when he was determined to be completely healthy, it was such a relief. We went to the coast with friends and life was really good. I felt so lucky to have my sweet baby and my fun toddlers. I was all set to teach three days a week, we had bought a great ranch-style house two years before, we had friends with small children too. Although I hadn't always wanted to be married to Will and he often ignored me when I spoke (I mean literally, as in I would say, "Guess what!" and he wouldn't even turn his head. As if I wasn't in the room. Ouch), I was content with my life. Sure, weekends were not easy because Will wouldn't spend time with our family, he wanted to be at the park with his friends bowling, playing pool, or smoking pot in the basement. But we were healthy, our home was pretty, and we had plenty of money.

It was about this time that I started taking antidepressants. New mothers often get post partum depression, and thankfully my mom noticed I was having trouble after Winston was born. Mainly, I wouldn't be able to get out of the house, I felt like everything had to be perfect first. I guess OCD is a good sign that a new mother's brain isn't functioning quite like it should be. Once I started taking a very small dose of medication I really felt like my life was coming together. But it was as though the more content I grew, the more discontent Will became. During my three month maternity leave he started coming home from work and grilling me about what I had done during the day, as if to make sure I had done enough to justify my staying home. As if caring for two toddlers and an infant and keeping the house picked up and meals prepared wasn't enough. He wanted me to do larger jobs too, like wash all the windows or reorganize files. I started keeping a list of the tasks I would complete on the white board in the kitchen, but it was never enough. He stopped coming to bed at night, he would stay up until one or two in the morning on his computer playing video games or, I suspect, looking at porn. I would beg him to come to bed, to talk to me, but he was unresponsive.

But I was busy and distracted and didn't have time to deal with him. He probably needed an antidepressant too, but I never will figure that out. When he would talk to me he spoke mainly of how he didn't get to go out and do fun things, how his friends were out golfing or bowling and he was stuck at home. His mantra seemed to be, "I never get to do anything *I* want to do." He said this throughout the day, whining, about having to be home whenever I asked him to eat dinner with us or accompany us anywhere.

Everything came to a head on November 1, ironic that this is the Day of the Dead, considering

I felt like everything we had died that day. It was a beautiful, unnaturally warm day, probably 60 degrees outside, brilliantly sunny and warm with all the leaves turing red and gold. After taking Sam and Cody to pre-school, I drove with Winston to my friend Maria's house and she and her two children and I met up with another friend and her two kids and we walked and walked and walked. It was a such a lovely day that we spend hours just walking around, pushing the strollers through the park and downtown and then back to Maria's house for tea. It was idyllic, the kind of day that made me want to be a full-time stay at home mom. Maria was on maternity leave at the same time as me and we laughed about becoming stay at home moms together.

When I returned home later that afternoon, I made dinner, put Winston down for a nap, put some clothes in the dryer, and picked up some toys. When Will came home about 3:30, I was in a calm and happy mood, and I greeted him from the kitchen table as he came through the back door from the garage. He did not smile back, he glowered and asked what I did that day. When I said I had gone on a walk with two friends and our kids it made him angry. He stomped through the house and said, "What the F- do you do all day?"

I felt my face grow hot with anger, I stood up and stormed downstairs into the basement and got clothes from the dryer and began stuffing them into the basket. I was doing two and three loads of laundry a day, usually one complete load just from Will. I seemed Will generated more clothing than the three kids and me put together, and I wondered sometimes if he was simply trying to create work for me. He had other things he did like that too - he would give two-year-old Sam and three-year-old Cody baskets and boxes of small toys, like those plastic Easter eggs or wooden blocks, then when they dumped them on the floor he would berate me for not picking them up. And I just took it. Silently seething but too afraid to speak up.

He had followed me downstairs and I started talking talking talking. Because, though I may have been a victim and mistreated, I was never weak or simpering. I can get mad and I can have a harsh tongue, and I started giving him a verbal lashing.

"What do I do all day? Huh? What do I do all day? Obviously nothing, I just sit on my fat butt and do nothing all day because I'm just lazy, that's what I do all day. I'm just a good for nothing!" I was talking furiously, spewing angry words as I grabbed the laundry basket full of clothes and brought it upstairs. He followed me into the dining room where I began to fold, angrily punctuating the folds with my monologue. He just stood there, glaring at me, but I didn't really pay attention to him. I was mad, I was mad at him for being a jerk when I was happy and for not appreciating me or our family and for criticizing me every day when staying home with small children is really hard work. I was mad because he would wear a shirt for two hours, with an undershirt and a sweatshirt and throw all three in the dirty clothes and then expect me to wash them even though they weren't dirty.

He yelled, "Shut the Fuck up!" and held his fist up as if he was going to punch me. I just got angrier.

"Oh yeah? You're going to punch me now? For not doing your laundry? Ha! Good one!" I wasn't even concerned about him, this is how safe I felt. This is how uninformed and blind I was.

I picked up the laundry basket and stalked into the bedroom to put his stupid clothes away. As I set the basket on the bed I heard the bedroom door slam behind me, I spun around to see what was happening and I knew.

I was in trouble.

Will's eyes were cold and dark and murderous, I couldn't even see him in there. I went from indignantly pissed off to hollowly terrified in an instant. Without a word I leaped for the phone. I picked it up and dialed 911, but before it even had a chance to ring he pulled the entire thing from the wall and threw it across the room. Then he came toward me. With both hands, he shoved me backwards, the force throwing me to the floor. He started yelling, but I wasn't hearing his words, I was silent and whimpering. I picked up a floor lamp and made one futile effort to escape, but he easily pulled the lamp from my hands and threw it across the room before shoving me down again. I was on the floor, face down, when he put both knees into my back and pushed my face to the floor, pulling my head awkwardly around, covering my mouth. He was still screaming, and I did hear his words now. I tried to break free, biting the fleshy part of his hand, which was over my mouth. He screamed in pain and pushed his knees more fiercely into my back, clasping both hands around my throat.

"Die, Bitch! Die!" He kept screaming this over and over as he squeezed harder and tighter around my throat. I got very calm and still here and, though I hadn't been to church very often in the previous years, I started saying the Lord's Prayer to myself in my head as everything started to go black. I said it twice through when I heard, over Will's chanting, Winston start to cry.

Will let go and got up, going to check on Winston. I dizzily jumped up and ran after him. Damn if he was going to hurt my baby. But he didn't, he seemed to be calm. He was looking in at the baby. And I calmly, as if nothing had just happened, said I should pick him up, he needed to nurse. Will let me, and then he even let me take Winston out onto the porch where I said he should

sit in the sunshine so he wouldn't get jaundice
again. Will was quiet, we sat silently for a
moment while the baby ate. Then Will left me
outside and went in. I could hear him inside,
freaking out in the bedroom, wailing about what a
mess it was. I knew things were still absolutely
not OK. I set the baby in the grass and tiptoed just
inside the front door and grabbed my car keys,
then I dashed out, grabbed Winston, and sprinted
to my Suburban. I was just buckling Winston into
his seat in the back when Will came screaming out
of the house, faster than I ever imagined anyone
could move toward me. His eyes were crazy. I
pulled the vehicle door shut and locked it, jumping
through to the driver's seat. The passenger
window was open a little way, and Will put his
fingers in the window and tried to pull it down.

He screamed in, "If you leave me, I will hunt
you down and kill you!" and held on to the car as I
pulled away. He was still holding onto the side of
the Suburban as a Schwan's truck driver pulled
toward us, trying to pass. He screamed some
obscenities at her. She made eye contact with me
and I could see the terror in her eyes, matching my
own. I made the phone sign with my hand and

mouthed "Call the police" to her just before pulling away.

Unbelievably, Will managed to get into his own car and speed to Cody and Sam's preschool and was already there with both boys when I pulled up. More amazingly, he had also managed to call my mom and had calmly told her how I had flipped out on him. This I learned when I called my mom, frantic, after he took the boys, even though the teacher leaned in and whispered, "Did he hit you?" Neither one of us wanted to let Will take Cody and Sam but he insisted and we couldn't stop him. As he sped off with my two toddlers I raced behind him, though he was driving so fast I couldn't keep up. As I was driving, I called my mom, hysterical, to ask what she thought I should do.

"Amanda?" she sounded concerned before I even had a chance to speak. "What is happening? Will just called. He told me you had gone crazy. That you bit him! What is happening?"

"Mom! He took them! He tried to hurt me! He has the boys. Oh Mom, what should I - !" I screamed, driving as fast as I safely could.

She cut me off harshly, "Amanda! Calm down. Take a deep breath. Now!! You are in control of your behavior, relax and calm down. I can't even understand you. What did you do to Will?"

I took a deep breath and blew it out slowly. My voice still shaking, I managed to tell her briefly what had happened.

"Amanda, when he called me about ten minutes ago he told me you had freaked out for no reason. That you had attacked him, bit his hand. That he felt unsafe with you. Where are the boys?" She was clearly concerned, but I could tell she instantly believed me. I was stunned that Will would go so far as to call my mom and accuse me of attacking him!

"What! How is that possible?" I shouted, my heart beginning to pound again. "Ten minutes ago he was driving to pick up the boys - going like sixty miles per hour! How could he have called you at the same time?"

"He did. And he sounded calm. He told me you had freaked out on him, bit his hand, and taken the baby."

I felt a sheet of ice move down my body. Will truly was psychotic. Who would think to call someone in the middle of what we had just gone through - just to make me look bad? What was he going to do with my boys? Where was he!! I started to whimper again, my chin wobbling as I drove without direction, looking for his car and our sons.

"Where are you?" my mom continued, her voice still soothing and helpful, though concerned.

"I'm driving! I have the baby. I tried to pick up the boys but he took them!" My voice was high pitched and hysterical. The idea of my two small boys with their dad in his state of fury was nearly blinding me with fear.

"Amanda!" my mom snapped, not sounding at all sympathetic. "Control your voice! Go home, I'm sure he went home. Go home. But get ahold of yourself first. If he is calmly telling me that you are freaking out and you sound like this people will think YOU are the person to blame here. You are a good actress! Pull yourself together and go home. I'll meet you there."

I took a few deep breaths and mustered all my acting ability, and by the time I arrived back at my house I at least looked normal. Thank God, Will had brought Sam and Cody home, he was standing in the front yard when I pulled into the driveway. I jumped out and ran toward them, grabbing both boys and hugging them. He looked stunned and barely acknowledged me. As I was leading the boys back to my car to get the baby, my dad pulled up and jumped out. He looked scared, looking between Will and me, taking in the scene. My tear-streaked face. The boys wide-eyed. Will pale with shock.

The police arrived a few minutes later, followed by my dad. The police had been called not only by the Schwan's truck driver but also by the preschool. My mom had sent my dad over. Being me, my main concern now that my children and I were safe, was to protect my unraveling reputation. I didn't want any of the neighbors to see a police car parked in front of my house and when they started to question me I glossed over most of it, claiming most of the responsibility ("Oh, I hadn't gotten the laundry done, I've just been lazy lately, he didn't mean it.") When the police kept referring to a "victim" I didn't know who they were talking about, and I was surprised when I asked and they told me it was me. I was the victim.

It took me a few days to acknowledge that I was in a bad situation and needed to leave. Thank goodness for our town's well-informed and respectful police officers who told me that I was a victim of domestic abuse and that I needed to get out or it most certainly would escalate. One policeman also returned to my house later to tell me again how important it was for me to leave the bad situation as well as to give me the phone number of the domestic abuse line at the YWCA. The YWCA was also very helpful, and it was the counsellor there who gave me the truest understanding of why I needed to leave.

"Do you want you sons to grow up to be abused?" She asked me that night when I called the number.

"No!" I practically shouted.

"Do you want your sons to be abusers?"

"Of course not!"

"This is what will happen if you stay with a man who abuses you. Your children will think it is OK for men to treat women this way, or even to be treated this way themselves. The only way to break the cycle is to walk away."

So, even though it was extremely difficult, I left. I left my beautiful home and plenty of money and comfortable life and hid out in a tiny room in my aunt's house. I endured people gossiping about me, expressing deep interest only to never speak to me again after hearing my story. I had many friends never invite me to do anything ever again. I was instantly destitute. I was so scared he would be true to his promise of hunting me down and killing me that I didn't sleep well for nearly a year. I have never been skinnier or more nervous, and not a good skinny either. I looked as pathetic as I felt.

But with time things have evened out. Will eventually managed to get his life in order well enough where the kids can now go stay with him for the weekend twice a month, and they love him and enjoy being with him. I lived with family for 6 years, but finally managed to buy another home - not too far from the one we had bought together all those years before. And though men have made me extremely uncomfortable for a long time, I dated on occasion and eventually met someone I could trust enough to let him meet my kids. We'll see where that goes.

I wonder sometimes what the purpose of all that ever was, if that great big mess that was my marriage has anything positive to offer the world. Of course, my kids, yes. But the other part, the ten years of marriage part. Will I ever be able to look back and just remember the good? The silly word games we would play, the three week road trip to Arkansas in the VW van, sharing the newspaper over breakfast in the morning? It's such a shame that our last fiery day together overwhelms the other 12 years we were together. I hope some day that bad afternoon can fade further into the recesses of my mind leaving me with happier memories of my marriage.

Day 25

Day 25

I return to work in one week and I am terrified.
I still can't really go out in public without a lot of
anxiety, even the grocery store makes me really
upset. Today I went grocery shopping and the
store was really crowded. I dealt with it by putting
on my big, dark, prescription sunglasses and
plugging earphones into my ears. I didn't see
hardly anyone I knew - though I did spot a student
(nice) and a coworker (also nice) from school. I
stayed out of their sight line and didn't have to talk

to either. I was friendly and polite, even chatty, with the butcher and the checkout lady. I took my glasses off and removed my headphones so I could be polite. But it still made me really uncomfortable. Later, the psychiatrist asked me, "What will happen to you, in these public situations? Why is it so bad?" and I could only tell him that I'm afraid I might get upset or start crying again. I might freak our or have a meltdown. He reminded me that I don't, I won't.

The worst thing about this is I don't feel this is me. Six months ago I was not this person, at all. I was totally social and confident, not at all afraid of these pubic spaces or having to make conversation with people. What happened? Sure, I have some old hurts - who doesn't? And probably much worse hurts than mine - so what if I had an ex-husband with a temper? So what if I got a divorce and didn't do super well at work? So what if the next guy I tried to date was, though kind, uncommitted? These are not reasons to freak out, to break down, to check out of life so thoroughly. Not at all, not even a little bit - wait, I think I might need to stop judging myself. I am doing so much better now than a month ago. I am totally sober; off of "helpful" medication, healthy and dealing with old stuff that I have buried for a long time.

And if I'm afraid to go back to work, that is probably justified. This has been a really lonely and stressful year, we got a new principal who decided to put me out in a horrible portable teaching a new grade level. I want to be good at what I do but I found myself struggling to be a good teacher and unhappy in an uncomfortable environment far from my usual teaching team. And something is wrong in my brain, something assures me - snidely and quietly - that they are all laughing at my failure. That I was once a talented teacher but now I don't even know how to work with the grade level they put me in. That this new principal who I barely know but who I have cried in front of multiple times in the past six months, will do anything to get rid of me. That our previous principal who I barely know either because he was only in our school for two years, must have heard I am bipolar and mentally ill and told her to make my job uncomfortable so I'll leave. And then no one will want me. And I'll flounder around from job to job, from school to school, for the 25 years I have left with the school district. My abilities and talents scorned and unseen.

But worse, it's not so much the school jobs that bother me so much, really, is it? It's the total failure, at the age of 39. My artistic endeavors, all those paintings, that no one wants to buy or look at. Or at least, if they want to see my at they just want to do it for free on social media. Because artists and creative people deserve to be poor, homeless, beggars. This is my true fear, isn't it? This idea that I will flounder around, moderately successful but not valued, as a school teacher for the rest of my life and I will never really chase my real dreams because I can't seem to let go of the stability of a satisfactory job. So I reach, desperate, like someone trying to cross monkey bars reaching toward the next bar - just out of reach - but unable to take the leap and actually let go. Unable to move on.

And why would I let go? So I have a career that feels stagnant and stifled and even cloying, but at least my union allows me to continue. Right, because I should be fired for being so sad and weepy that last day. For not being able to handle my last class of the day when that boy decided not to do any work, who told me to fuck off and who refused to leave the classroom when I asked him to leave, who yelled and laughed while I tried to teach Spanish to the rest of the students. And when the principal sneered at me, and rolled her eyes at the secretary, and laughed about my inability to understand their new discipline procedures. My heart breaks when I think of it, I'm so embarrassed to return. Who knows what they have said about me to other people. Who knows what that story has turned into - stupid Amanda crying in the office because she can't handle a hyper boy. Such terrible management skills. Such a bad teacher. So useless. Leave her in that portable that no one wants to be in. Let's give her the worst possible students next year, then maybe she really will quit.

So aren't these the thoughts of a depressed woman? Right, I read my own words and I think of how bleak they are. How pathetic and overdramatic, just like my inability to go to the grocery store without anxiety. I need to be kinder to myself, somehow. Maybe I should get dressed

and see if my love will go to that square dance
with me. Turn off the TV. Take a shower. ACT
like I'm not depressed until I am not depressed.

Day 26

Day 26

Still sober and no medication (except sleeping pill). Yay me!

Thank God I got up off the couch last night and did something social and active. I dragged my love to that dance and actually had a good time. Of course, it was pretty low-key, almost everyone there was retirement age. Since it was a square dance there was no time to make conversation - I avoided the dreaded, "Are you OK?" questions.

So perfect. I realize this is the first social situation in almost a month that I have been in and not felt incredible nervous. Easing into this easily is the way to go. And to think I used to be so very, very social. To the scary extreme.

I remember the night last summer when I went to the Solstice celebration with Maria at her cousin's farm. It was mid-summer, the hottest days of the year. I started out all right, sipping beer and chatting with all of my new acquaintances, wading in the river. But as the night continued on and everyone started moving off to their tents to go to bed I just got more and more wild. Dancing around the fire as two guys I had just met played their guitars, singing. A third guy, I think his name was Dan or maybe Don, he joined me as I danced. I ended up grabbing his hand and pulling him into the bushes, kissing him hungrily.

We tumbled onto the ground and rolled around for a few minutes until he whispered in my ear that he had a condom in his car, let's go. I snapped into reality, remembering my love at home asleep. Laughing I got back up and grabbed his hands, pulling him back to the fire. Such was our drunkenness that he didn't even seem to mind my dismissal. The other two guys hadn't even noticed we'd left, they were still playing music.

The bad thing was, about five minutes later an angry looking woman burst out of the same bushes we had crashed through.

"You slut!" she had yelled at me.

By that time I was clapping along to the guitar, not even thinking about Dan (or Don). I looked up at her furious face and felt fear and confusion. I had spoken to her briefly, her name was Pattie. She was a pretty successful local musician who I had read about a few times in the paper.

"What?" one of the guitar players stopped playing abruptly and looked at her in confusion.

She pointed fiercely at me, "This whore just had sex right next to my daughters tent."

I was dumbstruck, I couldn't even think of what to say. But the other guitar player had also stopped playing at this point and joined in the drama, saying, "What are you talking about Pattie, she's been here the whole time."

Pattie rolled her eyes and threw one more wrathful comment my way, "Next time you decide to FUCK someone, don't do it right next to my daughter's tent!"

As she stomped back through the bushes I looked around, not sure if I should confess or if she had even been talking about me - our brief tumble could hardly qualify as sex. When I looked at my partner in crime he looked equally disturbed and confused, shaking his head and shrugging. The other two, who must not have even noticed our brief absence, just laughed and went back to playing music.

The four of us stayed up the rest of the night, singing and talking, laughing at every small thing. One of the guitar players, his name was Ted, told us that he was bipolar and often ended up being the only one left at parties. I laughed my head off at this, finding it so funny because I was the same way. Later on another girl walked out to our campfire. At least this woman was more kind, she politely told us it was 4:30 and we were so loud she was having trouble sleeping. After this we all calmed down a little before finally going to our different tents as the night was turning gray and morning birds were starting to call.

A few hours later, when I woke up as refreshed and cheerful as ever despite very little sleep and a ton of beer, I saw Pattie glaring at me. Her twelve year old daughter was also glaring at me. Great.

Day of the Dead: The Prequel

It's funny how November 1ˢᵗ was the date that my ex-husband chose to freak out on our family since there there was another Day of The Dead, a few years before that evil and violent Day of The Dead when things were quite different.

This was before my kids were born, back when I had been a young and innocent college student. At that time Carlisle hadn't yet become the famous as the drummer for The Flying Foes. He was just a cute guy that had given me a surprise kiss the previous spring.

I guess it wasn't really November 1st when it started, it was Halloween, and I was in one of my manic states. Halloween. I looooooove Halloween. That year was the best ever, too, because it was on a Friday. It was a fantastic day at at school. I had dressed as a cowgirl, we'd had a party in my English Composition class. I drank three cups of coffee and ate a handful of nuts. I hadn't been able to eat or hardly even drink for two days. I was living off of hot water, coffee, and peanuts.

Then the evening. I lit my Octoberfest Jack-O-Lantern, dressed as a Treasure Chest Dancer, and partied at Al, Dax, and Tom's house with a few of kids from school: Jody, Phil, Jim, Alfie. Al brought Crown Royale. Erica drew a star on my face and another on my belly. We went trick-or-treating, annoying the neighbors.

Then to the bar scene (after a quick toke session). At Henderson Bar it was surprisingly tranquil and quiet. We played pool and took pictures. A group of guys from school showed up as rockstars, that was funny. While standing at the bar ordering a beer Carlisle came up to me. He actually approached me, the first time since that party where he kissed me. He said hello and talked to me for a minute. He was dressed like Richie Tennenbaum the tennis star from The Royal Tennenbaums with a white tennis getup and a headband. He looked cuter than ever.

I was wearing black knee-high leather zip up Fly boots with a 6-inch heel. I had on a grey leather jacket with a fur collar, which I was too embarrassed to take off in a quiet bar. Underneath I had on a white midriff tank top, a gray cashmere sweater that was way too small, thigh-high silk stockings, a gold garter belt, black boy underwear, and a sheer dancer skirt. My butt cheeks were clearly visible - hence the long leather coat. I also wore a cross necklace, a black messenger boy hat and the two stars drawn on my face and stomach. Definitely too risqué for The Henderson.

But not too revealing for Funky Town, which we somehow decided to go to an hour later. I have never seen that place so crowded. It was so hot and full of partiers no one even noticed when I took off my coat - well maybe Carlisle did, I caught him looking at me from across the room. I guess I might have been trying to make him jealous when I shared a sucker with George from my Bio class. And when I danced with those two guys from California, what were their names? And when I shared that beer with Al. Oh and Josh Thatcher and Rick Hollis and AJ from English Comp. And Zach Emerson dressed like a pimp with a white fur coat and sunglasses. And Chad as The Phantom of the Opera. And Erica as Little Red Riding Whore. Shari as Wednesday Adams. But never Carlisle. I just watched him from the corner of my eye as he stood at the back of the bar with his arms crossed, looking at me.

So the night continued on, crowds, difficulty moving from the bar to the dance floor to the bathrooms. While standing at the bar, Carlisle came next to me again and he bought me a drink. Wow. He never bought me drinks. He was sober, too. We talked a bit, but I liked him so much he made me nervous and uncomfortable. After awhile I began to worry less about impressing him or if he still liked me after that random kiss we never talked about.

Then Funky Town closed - I hate that when two'o-clock rolls around and they abruptly turn on the lights and turn off the music and suddenly I'm surrounded by drunk men trying desperately to score. Why does two in the morning always have to come so quickly? I stood next to him outside. He said I was like a magnet. What did that mean? I only talked to him briefly all night. A magnet. Of course I laughed. Everything made me laugh all night. He said he was walking with Zach and set off without saying goodbye.

I left with Jody, Jim, Alfie, Chad, and Rick. As we went to get into the car, three other guys started getting in. Something about being piled, seatbeltless and drunk, into a car driven by a drunk man I couldn't even identify seemed wrong to me, so I jumped out. I walked toward Carlisle and Zach. Even though Jody and everyone yelled after me, I just waved and kept walking until I caught up with them.

I held Carlisle's arm (Zach's too when he wasn't on the phone trying to score) as we walked like six blocks to Carlisle's car. Aaaaaaahhhhhh.....45 minutes of Carlisle's company was really great. He mentioned a couple of times that I seem to know everything about him. That's weird. It's been almost four months since we had any kind of meaningful connection. I said (aloud, why? Oh drunkenness! Craziness!) that maybe I'm so interested in him because we are going to die together. He acted mad at that, but not really, asking if I was going to kill him and myself too? No way.

We got to his car and Zach grabbed my arm and tried to be all smooth, coming on to me. None of his other hook-ups must have panned out. I pulled away and laughed, but Carlisle glared at him and told him to let me sit in the front. Zach slid into the front anyway. I was already in the back at that point, but I was impressed by Carlisle's sweetness. The three of us sat in Carlisle's car for probably ten minutes while we waited for it to get warm. Carlisle put on music by one of his obscure groups. Zach kept reaching back and touching me, trying to be sexy, but not really succeeding. He was rubbing my wrist but doing it all wrong - hard and fast. What is it with men who think hard and fast is the way to go with women?

Anyway, I said, "Not like that, like this," and tried to show him how to use a soft touch on the back of his hand. Why? I guess being dressed like a hooker makes me flirtatious. But Zach still didn't get it.

Carlisle asked grumpily what we were doing. Irritated. Zach my hat off my head and threw it up front. I grabbed my hat, reaching around and trying to touch Carlisle. He said my fingers were cold but wouldn't flirt with me, he just put the car in gear and started driving. He didn't ask where I was going, just drove to my apartment and dropped me off. Me first, not Zach.

I tried to pretend I didn't care. I jumped out and cheerfully said. "Thank-you, Happy Halloween!"

Why was he always so interesting to me? I don't know if I liked him or just liked teasing him. Or was it that he was the only guy who didn't seem to like me. I liked making him mad, I wanted him to think about me and suffer, like I'd suffered for him. I wanted him to love me. I wanted him to pine away with desire for me.

No, that's harsh. I never really wished any sad or difficult feelings on Carlisle. I honestly just felt a connection to him and wished he felt the same way. Who knows, maybe he did? Maybe. He felt something about me, I know this since he never just ignored me. He even sought me out a couple of times and stood talking to me. He stood next to me and bought me a drink. He gave me his arm when we walked. He teased me pretty persistently about my middle name when I told him - he must have said Amanda Jane 3 or 4 times when we were walking to his car. He drove me home. I don't think I mean nothing to him.

Be Honest

Day 26, after my psychiatric appointment.

My psychiatrist told me yesterday that I need to tell people I missed work because I got depressed. We practiced what I will say when I go back to work: I got depressed. I sought help. I'm much better. Thank you. (And stop, don't tell more. Plus be sincere when I say thank-you). I pushed back, insisting I should tell people I had a bad reaction to medication. Or just let people think I got into a car wreck. Or....or....

Dr. Reed had burst out, "Amanda! Stop trying to control what other people think!"

"But - but....they'll think I'm crazy! They'll judge me! They say I'm not safe to teach! Mentally unstable!" I blubbered, the tears returning.

"Fuck 'em!" he roared, "that's their problem. Be honest about who you are, Amanda, or you'll stay fragile and nervous forever. Be proud of who YOU, Amanda Jones, are! If they judge you, don't make it your problem. Analyze them with cold calculation. Are they concerned about their own mental health? Or do they harbor a deep hidden cruelty that they can't keep from coming forth? It's not your problem. All you need to worry about is what YOU think, you can't control them. Just keep your center and be honest about who you are."

I reeled back, before bursting out laughing. Sure, fuck 'em.

And I thought of the last person who had lashed out at me and how I had allowed that happened.

My mind drifts back to Sonara. Scary how she got meaner and meaner, and like with Will, I didn't defend myself or walk away when she started to unfairly criticize me or cut me down. How I even let her yell at me and only told myself I deserved it instead of standing up to myself. Why would I let this happen?

I gave and give and all she did was take until I had nothing left. She screamed at me that I'm selfish and crazy and I sat mute, never one time defending myself. Barely able to speak, certainly not able to stand up and tell her she was mistreating me. How I left and cried and contemplated suicide for a week, thinking she must be right. I am selfish and condescending and talk too much. My family would be better off without me..

Acupuncture helped a little, the acupuncturist soothingly reminding me that I can't give to the point of being taken advantage of, I need to get away from unstable people. I was victimized because I allowed it. Not because I deserved it.

But maybe I feel I deserve it. I detest myself, disgusting Amanda, so much, I just wish I could die sometimes. But just as quickly I feel bad for thinking horrible things about myself mainly because my parents and kids and my brother seem to actually like me - if I hate myself so much, it is like spitting on them. Calling them stupid for having faith in my value.

And then I remember I'm mentally ill.

There is something intrinsically wrong with me. My mind doesn't function correctly. Oh, and I'm an alcoholic, that never helps matters. So what if people go on social media and post how mental illness is OK!! It is just a health problem blah blah blah…But those of us with mental health problems stay quiet. Because we know. We know when that guy with a heart disease has a heart attack people might blame his diet, but no one is going to gossip about what a loser he is. Gleefully gossip, I might add…right mom? The diabetic gets cranky, maybe, but he also loses limbs and eyesight. And no one is going to scream at him that he needs to adjust his medication! Get help! Without even knowing anything about their actual health care.

The epileptic has a seizure. The cancer victim gets weak and thin. But me? Other people with mental illness? Ha! Ha ha ha ha hahahahahahahaha!!!!!! It's not that clear. I freak out. It may be hard to believe because I seem like a stable steady person as I go about my regular day as a mom and teacher and upstanding community member. I hold it together really well, most of the time, with my big smile and friendly conversation. But give me enough time without medication or on the wrong medication, mix that with a few sleepless nights, and KAZAM!! I am a movie star, oh yeah! I go to one party and talk and laugh and talk and laugh and talk and laugh until everyone else (except other people who are manic and also people on coke and meth) goes to bed.

I pretend to yawn too! But I don't go home… I go to the next party! And the next!! And the next!!! Ha ha ha! I go and I go and I go until the sun comes up…then I go to work. Hee hee! I tell stories and jokes and smile and laugh. I'm crazy popular. Wild eyed. Not myself. For days and weeks. I get skinny and twitchy. I look like a tweaker except I have never used crack or meth or coke or anything. Or maybe I look how I'm supposed to look because everyone loves skinny laughing women with long blonde hair and cute clothes.

Eventually something happens - help arrives in the form or medication or someone screaming at me or just a regular ol' crash. Then I trudge away. Embarrassed and ashamed, suicidal and full of loathing and darkness. Quiet, tired, sad, prone to tears and tragic proclamations.

If I stay on the medicine, whichever teeny-tiny pill the doctor most recently suggested, I am pretty good. Maybe more on the dark sad side, but no one loathes me. Well, I loathe me, but what does that matter? They loathe that dancing, singing, table jumping, name memorizing talker. Or maybe they love that wild girl. Maybe only I hate her. So I stay on the little pills, depending on how bad I've gotten. And more importantly I stay quiet. Because I've learned the hardest way that people carry cruelty around when they know a person has a reviled illness like mine. Any mis-step, any grumpy or irritated word, any laugh that lasts too long and people who know my secret might blast me with, "Adjust your medication!" Like Sonara

did after she listed every flaw I have. After I
ALLOWED her to tell me every flaw I have. Like
I'm permanently broken. Unable to show emotion,
eagerness, sadness, ever again.

And who can blame Sonara? My emotions can
get out of hand. The laughter can escalate into
insane hysteria. The tears can lead to endless
sobbing. Of course people are scornful, Amanda,
control yourself you stupid schizo.

Day 27: Think Positive

Day 27

I wonder if all this wallowing actually helps me feel better? I doubt it. Here I am, just a few days until I have to return to work, nearly at DAY 30 - healed! - and I'm still thinking about all that crap from so long ago? I need to move on!! As my brother helped me rake leaves out of flower beds this morning, I thought about how far I've come, how far my brother has come too. Maybe, like all the rotting leaves covering up the tiny new early spring buds, the old stuff needs to be moved away before new life can come in.

Poor Charlie, he'd really gone through some sad times when his wife had left him. He had been blindsided. We all had. They had been (we all thought) happily married for seven years, living on forty acres of dry land wheat, a pond, horses, a dog, and two cats. His wife, Rachel, hadn't wanted to have children and had been very motivated to succeed in her business classes and later as a bank executive, but he had figured eventually she would want to settle down a little and have a couple of children. We would talk about how fun it would be for my boys to have cousins. But time had passed and she had just become more and more interested in being successful at her career. Making a lot of money had become her passion and Charlie had noticed that she began losing interest in their home. She started coming home from the bank later and later and had, one disturbing evening after the office Christmas party, not come home at all. The hardest thing for Charlie was that she had barely spoken to him about the end of their marriage, though her lawyer had plenty to say. After a year of arguing through the courts and letter written by lawyers, he had finally been legally free of Rachel, though emotionally he was torn up. Financially too, having to sell his farmland to pay her off. We worried about him for a long time.

For awhile there we were a good team. I was a divorced disaster who managed to keep it together. And he was much less of a mess, but still in the same boat. Even though he was good looking and was able to buy a great house and was a successful contractor he hadn't been able to find love. He had tried, but he hadn't been able to meet the right woman. I always suspected he couldn't forget Erica. And who wants to hold a torch for a famous singer, even if they had cared about each other when they were young? I knew how that hurt with Carlisle.

So he tried to meet other girls, we all fixed him up with anyone we could think of. But so many women just seemed to want him for his money. Or because they were frantically searching for a husband and any man would do. Or they were just collecting men. I started thinking both Charlie and I would just be single for the rest of his life.

Charlie and I had dinner together at least weekly, usually with my parents and always with my kids. I've always felt lucky to have such a great big brother. We probably could have enjoyed that time better. But I always ended up wallowing around, worrying about Will and then later Dex. And Charlie would sadly lament how he just wanted someone who knew him, who loved him for himself. Though he was always stronger than me and eventually seemed to settle into a happy routine. After awhile we didn't even talk about dating anyone. Why wallow in pain? He hadn't cared for Dex, though he had certainly liked him better than Will. And he never even bothered to introduce any women he might have briefly dated.

Then, suddenly, things worked out for both of us. The circumstances were terrible - Erica's bandmate Jim Jackson had died in a terrible accident (OK, it was a heroin overdose). We were all reeling with the shock and sadness of losing our friend. But somehow the time that followed was a magical mixture of endings and beginnings. It was last spring, that sparkling time right before summer arrives. Erica had come home to recuperate and she and Charlie ended up spending in all their free time together. And then Penny told me Carlisle had joined her. He arrived with his older sister, Jenna, and Jenna's husband Ben, who was the bassist for The Flying Foes. I tried to play it cool, but the moment Penny told me he was in town I knew I had to see him. Even if it was just for a moment, even if he was still mad at me, even if he brought that model with him...I couldn't wait until I saw him again.

Of course, it wasn't a good situation, at all. We had all loved Jim. Who wouldn't? There was a reason he was one of the most famous musicians of our time: funny, friendly, gorgeous, and supremely talented. I couldn't believe he'd hidden a heroin addiction, though I myself had hidden issues - I certainly had never told any of my friends my doctor and counsellor had both diagnosed me with bipolar disorder. Like me, Jim probably didn't want to worry anyone. I wish we had known, maybe we could have helped him somehow. All of us were still reeling from the loss. But now that his band mates were in town we were all finding comfort just being together. Even though no one really wanted to talk about Jim and his death, we had all seen the tabloids; I knew Carlisle had been with him the night he died.

I had tried to forget Carlisle for so long. After our one magical/disastrous night and then seeing him engaged to Simone, I had avoided even looking at magazines if they were about the Foes. I didn't want my heart to break any more. And I figured he'd forgotten about me anyway.

Until the night The Flying Foes played their tribute to Jim. Penny, Geri and I got to Main Street Studios early so we could get one of the good tall tables in front. I hadn't seen Carlisle since he'd returned to town, but I was very aware that he would be there. My friends had stayed thankfully quiet about him, even though I knew they suspected my feelings for him had never changed. As people started to pour into the candle-lit room, talking and laughing, I felt a small tap on my arm. Turning around I was happy to see Jenna, Carlisle's big sister. She was with Kelly Jackson, Jim's wife - widow. I gave Kelly a small, sympathetic smile. Though I could see her eyes were red from crying she still smiled back bravely.

None of us would ever be the same after Jim, but Kelly was dealing with the aftermath much more than any of us could imagine. Jenna kept her arm protectively around Kelly as they joined us.

"Amanda!" Jenna said as she gave me a big hug, giving Geri and Penny big hugs too. Her bright blue eyes sparkled as she gave my arm an extra squeeze.

"Carlisle will be so glad you're here," she said, giving me a warm smile.

My heart had thudded in my chest. Had he been thinking of me all these years too? I scanned the room for Simone, had he brought her? Were they together? No, Jenna had said he'd be glad I was here. Did he still care?

Before I had a chance to ponder this heartwarming idea I heard Erica's bright laughter from the stage. They were starting! The crowd quickly quieted, immediately enthralled with Erica's sparkling stage presence. As I looked at my childhood friend-turned-rock-star I couldn't help but smile. Erica Princeton has always been larger than life, even when she is grieving her best friend's overdose.

And despite the circumstances, the three remaining Flying Foes sounded great! And more surprisingly, my big brother ran out and joined them after their first three songs. Erica looked beautiful dancing up on stage, her face was lit up in a smile as she looked over at Charlie singing along with her. I could tell the crowd loved it. In the three weeks we had been home Erica had been spending a lot of time with Charlie. He had been playing the guitar and singing with her, Carlisle, and Ben. The two songs he had played with the group had been excellent and I could tell the crowd enjoyed him.

Then Erica had spoken directly to us, her usually sunny face etched in a grief that pulled at my soul.

"This one is dedicated to our dear friend, Jimmy. We love you Jim and we send this one up to you."

The song was slow, a beautiful ballad completely different from what The Flying Foes had always been famous for, but in the same way still shining with their signature freedom and spirit. Everyone in the room seemed to hold their breath as Erica, Ben, and Carlisle played. I tried not to stare at Carlisle as he played his drums softly, but each time I saw him singing along, harmonizing with Erica, his eyes closed, my hear just soared. I looked down, feeling foolish. I couldn't be starstruck over this man! I knew him too well and too much had happened between us.

I looked away just in time to see a guy we had gone to school with, Raymond something, approach Penny. She lit up in a way I had never seen as she gave him a little hug. Hmmmm....I glanced at Geri who had also seen the exchange and we both dissolved into laughter. Raymond and Penny? I could hardly remember him from school but from the look on her face Penny sure hadn't forgotten him. I turned back to the stage and kept my eyes away from Carlisle for the rest of the song. Seeing my friend connecting with someone made me yearn for a real love, one like I'd only heard about but never gotten to experience. The song finished and I quickly wiped the tears that were beginning to form in my eyes, shaking my head at my own sentimentality.

Erica told us she needed to take a breather and then jumped lithely down from the stage and joined us. I could feel the audience watching her and I couldn't help but feel proud that we were her true friends, the people she chose to join for her break.

"Amanda! I'm so glad you're here," Erica murmured into my ear as she gave me a big hug.

As I was returning her hug I felt the small hair on the back of my neck tingle. I could feel Carlisle looking at me before I saw him standing behind Erica. I met his strong gaze briefly before looking down shyly. I hadn't seen him in so long yet I could immediately feel our chemistry. When I looked back up he was still staring at me intently. I noticed his full lips and blushed, looking away again. What if Carlisle's beautiful girlfriend were here too? I briefly looked around the room for Simone again, relieved I didn't see her.

I heard his deep, smooth voice before I realized Carlisle was now standing right behind me. I turned toward him and felt my face break into a huge smile.

"Did you pay the bartender for the extra candle?" he asked, looking at the two flickering candles on our table.

Without thinking I reached for my purse, flustered by his intense gaze, "Oh! I hadn't realized..."

His mock concern melted into a wide smile, his eyes still on mine. I could feel my whole body tingling as I laughed. Carlisle had always loved teasing me.

"Carlisle! You always could get me!" I said, my nervousness melting away as I gave him a big hug.

"Will you come outside with me?" he said in his slow, calm way.

I nodded mutely, taking his hand. My heart was pounding and I couldn't even breathe as I followed him through the crowd.

Once we got outside on the front patio, he pulled me away from the smokers to a quiet space near a potted tree and looked intensely at me.

"Are you having a good night?" he asked, though the heat between us made it clear he wasn't interested in meaningless conversation. He was still holding my hand and he pulled me closer, pulling my hand up to his chest.

As I stepped into him I had to tilt my head back to look into his eyes. His blue eyes were calm and decided.

"Aren't you supposed to be engaged or something?" I asked him softly, running my hand gently over his blue flannel shirt until I could feel his heart beating.

"Amanda, there has only ever been you," he said quietly before he kissed me.

I kissed him back briefly, feeling immediately the spark we had shared all those years before, before stepping back slightly.

"But the tabloids, the engagement…" I said, shaking my hand.

He pulled me toward him again, now putting his hand on my back.

"Simone is gay. We are friends, you'll meet her. She's great," he whispered, his lips tickling my ear.

I looked at him and saw his sincerity and I realized I was done pushing people away. I was done looking. I was done worrying about love. My love was here. I laughed put my arms around him, breathing in deeply as he held me in a tight hug.

"Carlisle!" Ben Beirne, the bassist for the Foes was standing in the doorway, completely unconcerned that we were displaying some very public affection two feet away.

Carlisle kept his arm around me and looked at his friend, "Is it time?" he asked in his cool way.

Ben winked at me and I smiled back, dipping my head into Carlisle's shoulder. Carlisle gave me a kiss on the forehead and led me back inside so he could go back up on stage and be a rock star.

Day 28: Facing Reality

Day 28

I feel so good. So healthy. Of course there is
always that pessimistic side of me that whispers
that it's because the sun has returned and the first
hints of spring are now here, that next winter I'll
just tumble down down down again. But then I
swim back to my true self and feel my strength and
know I am in a new place, different than ever
before. My love, Carlisle, is such a solid rock for
me. My boys are so loving and happy. My family

is near by. I am healthy. I have so much to be thankful for.

Although there is still reality. My job, my high school teaching job, which I've studiously avoided thinking about all this time. My best friend Maria. The administration that puts me in a portable far from all the other language teachers, far from any other teachers. Maria. My last class of the day with not one, not two, not three, but four kids with severe behavior problems. Why are kids who are prone to screaming meltdowns all taking Spanish? The last class of the day? All together? It's a nightmare. Then my thoughts drift inexorably back to Maria, the last time we talked, my failure to help her. I wish she was alive.

One month ago I was still reeling from her death. Still thinking about it every time my mind was not actively distracted by something else. I would talk to her when my classroom was empty, wishing she could hear me.

"I miss talking to you, my friend, if for no other reason than I know you would not probably have really enjoyed teasing me about how obsessed I am about your death. If you weren't soaked in chemicals and stuffed in a ten-thousand dollar box dressed in - what? What were you wearing in that closed casket? How does one decide what to put a gorgeous 37-year old woman in before burying her? Did they buy you a black dress, even though you never wore black? Or were you even in that coffin? Maybe they were lying to us, they just cremated you. Or did they get you all beautiful before closing you up inside? Did they put you in your favorite purple pant suit, maybe wrap your huge blue scarf around your neck, since your neck was maybe broken, or at least rope burned or bruised?

Who found you? How did you do it, exactly? And more importantly, WHY? Why Maria? What compelled you to go out, buy a rope, research knots, tie it to - where? Tie your head into it and - what? Jump? Kick a chair out from under yourself? Were your kids home? I have to think they were not. Why did your stupid ex-husband not talk to me, to any of us? Just shuffling his guilty feet and looking at the floor when we came in, clutching your poor daughters' hands. Why didn't they tell us more in the newspaper? Why didn't the school tell us anything? They just expected us to hop back into our lives, as if nothing had happened. The principal acting surprised when I started crying at the staff meeting the next week, asking me why I was so upset. It didn't even occur to her that I might be upset about you. Why was this not a huge deal!?! Your students were the most susceptible to struggles, with their poverty and incentives to join gangs. The last day we spoke, eating our lunches in the staff room, you not really eating because you were so stressed out, you told me you were depressed. You told me! And I failed you. You couldn't get over your ex-husband's betrayal, your looming poverty, your children having to spend time with him even when he had always been too busy to talk to them before. Add that to your former student writing to you from jail, apologizing for killing your cousin? No one would have been able to endure. But I had failed you. I hadn't realized the extent of your pain. I had tried to reassure you, to suggest a girls weekend, like that would have helped you at that time.

Oh Maria. Why did you kill yourself?"

My last day, when all four of my 7th period behavior problem kids all decided to have their own private freak out session while I tried to teach beginning verb conjugation? I would have marched to Maria's room instead of to the office. She would have stopped me from bursting in to that office and asking the principal why no one had sent in someone to help me escort at least one kid from my room. When I cried Maria would have soothed my agitation by listening and sympathizing, certainly offering an even worse story from her classes which are always loaded with many more behavior problems than my own classes. She would have listened and given me the strength and confidence to confront the useless principal in a productive way, instead of with tears already streaking down my face as I thought of Joe screaming at me to fuck off before he decided to leave class early. As I thought of Lily giving her own thumb a blow job while looking across the room at Edward. As I thought of Mathew refusing to sit down while yelling at me that he hates Spanish. All as I sat with my ear to the phone, trying to reach the office so I could warn them that Joe was now roaming the halls, furious.

Is this why everything fell apart? I suppose it might be. It was at least the proverbial straw. Because that last day, when I walked away from that last class fighting back tears...I vowed to never return. And of course, teachers can't do that. We don't get to quit. We get to quietly endure. We get to stand up in front of class after class after class with a big cheery smile on our face as we deal with all of society's problems. But I marched away. No, I slunk away. I could barely see through my own tears after the principal reprimanded me for not filling out the proper form. Because, yes, forms are the important part.

I know I'm good at teaching: creative, innovative, cheerful, consistent. But all of this, piled together on top of crap from before: this past fall, a student's dad shot her mom then killed himself. A week later a colleague's son was stillborn, and a month after that, Maria. Somehow I just couldn't endure it. I lost my ability to keep it positive all the time, to smoothly remove oppositional teenagers who disrupt everyone's learning, to even feel adequate. Especially when the state demands 'evidence' that I am meeting instructional goals in an endless quagmire of documentation. All while taking a tiny pay cut each year as our insurance costs rise and our pay remains the same for the past twelve years. And my ex-husband doesn't help financially. And…and…and…

This past fall, when I hadn't been able to stop crying as I drove to my school everyday, I had asked my doctor for help. Anti-depressants and anti-anxiety drugs were supposed to numb the pain and stress. More and more anti (feeling) drugs didn't seem to work. I cried whenever I could all through the fall and winter. I faked it for my students and colleagues. Every free moment I had I searched for other jobs (like more stress would help - but hey, I was not thinking clearly). I endured administration who blamed me for not feeling better after my friend had killed herself. They acted like her death had nothing to do, at least partly, with working with hurt and impoverished students under cold bureaucratic scrutiny.

When my mind began searching for solutions and found none, awake all night worrying about the kids who come to school drunk (at age 14), the girls who I suspect are abused, the boy who flipped me off and ran out of class and then had no consequence because he wouldn't show up for detention…only frightening answers began to emerge. Like Maria a couple of months earlier, like another colleague two years ago, suicide started looking reasonable.

I shook it off, of course I'm not going to kill myself! My best friend killed herself and none of us will ever recover. Suicide is not the answer. Yet, late at night, I'd formulate plans. It seemed the only escape, no other job was coming my way. I didn't have enough money to pay for my own children's basic needs. I hadn't seen the sun in months. My best friend was gone and my other friends were busy or lived far away. I couldn't tell Carlisle for fear he'd flee in terror at my illness. And my job got more and more stressful. There seemed no way out. What else could there even be? Life used to be so hopeful!

When I found myself struggling to drive straight on the highway, talking myself out of running head-on into a semi truck. When my pills started to beckon, enticing me to eat them all at once. When I began to truly think of the steps it would take to hang myself too…I got scared. No job is worth this agony.

Now I think of how I walked away and I no longer felt anxious or upset. I had done what I needed to. I had asked my supervisor for help with one more behavior problem and she sneered at me. She told me I do not understand the discipline system. Fill out this form, that form. She offered nothing I could use to ease the turmoil. Is there a form for my orphan girl? Will the form help her? How about the kid whose parents are in a gang and don't take care of him? Which box do I tick off for getting help for him? And me? Is there a form that will ease my deep feelings of failure and inadequacy?

Before I had a chance to try out any of my methods for escape, I instead wisely got help. I went to the doctor, told her the ideas for killing myself. A medical team helped me, helped me wean off the anti-anxiety and anti-depressants so I could feel. And they told me to not go to school. Recover. Be well. See a counsellor. Of course, my insurance won't pay for any of this treatment. So my children and I will have to forgo - something, I don't even know what - to pay for it.

Now, almost a month later, I sleep. All night. Without medication. I feel hope again. I FEEL again. And suicide is never the answer, I don't just know this now. I actually believe it.

But I'm no longer teaching. I am afraid to return in a couple of days. I feel good now, but what will happen when I'm again thrust into an environment where so many people struggle and my colleagues and I are the culprits? How will I endure? I know how Maria chose to get out of it and I wish she hadn't killed herself. Just a week before I left I accidentally came across an email Maria had sent me just a few days before she died. I'd typed "court" into the search bar of my email so I could fill out a form for a kid who keeps skipping school and now is going to court. Instead this email came up:

From: TeacherMaria@hometownmail.com
To: TeacherAmanda@hometownmail.com
Subject: Edit?
September 15 at 2:55 PM

Thank you Amanda, the pot roast recipe was great! Both girls loved it.

Hey, would you edit the attached essay for me? One of those online teacher blogs asked me for my own personal account of working with struggling students. I think they will even publish it. Imagine, me - a writer! Anyway, just give it a quick read and let me know if it doesn't make sense or something.

Making a Difference

I am a bilingual special education teacher at a large high school. I see my students struggle daily to make their lives successful, many despite numerous personal obstacles. A girl at our high school killed herself this past week. Another former student shot her ex-boyfriend's new girlfriend after a drug deal went wrong. A former student shot a rival gang member's mother on her front porch. I read about my previous students on a regular basis in the court section of the newspaper: robbing stores, running from police, getting stopped for dealing drugs. Shooting each other in alleys. Shooting each other from their cars. Shooting each other at parties. It hurts to think too much about it.

How are these all tied together? What has happened to create this? I can only speculate based on observation, but I can tell you what all of the students have in common: Nearly all are the children or grandchildren of Mexican immigrants, they all live far below the poverty level, and they all have received a lot of "Differentiated Instruction" (i.e. being pulled out of class to be given remedial help). Do these things add up? I don't know, as the teacher providing the "special" education to these students I see first hand how they are not invited to participate in the mainstream, middle class, school system. They are kept separate. Does this make them angry? It makes me angry, so it wouldn't surprise me if they felt the same lack of connection to their community that I witness as one of their teachers.

And do you know where I live? A beautiful, lovely, upscale, expensive tourist town on the West Coast of the United States. There is sooooooo much wealth here. So many gorgeous mansions.

So many tourists throwing so much money into our economy every weekend as they eat $200 meals, buy $80 bottles of wine, and stay in upscale Bed and Breakfasts. We appreciate our tourist industry, we all hope to maybe get a small share of it. But the holders of wealth here, and all over our country, do what they can to contain it to just a few.

How does our population of lower-level earners, regardless of race, fare? I'm not sure I can say they do well, as a whole. Of course there are exceptions, but for many there is a disparity in income and social acceptance that creates a turbulence that our tourists never see. As tourists walk around "America's Best Downtown" and buy expensive trinkets, they don't get a chance to see our large homeless population. They don't think about the many workers who pick and process the grapes that go into their world class wine. They don't realize who is cleaning their room after they leave. Or maybe they do. I hope they do. I hope this all gets better.

What about teachers, how do we fare? We still manage to do well, though it gets harder and harder for us to buy houses or pay for medical care or food. I have taken a 10% pay cut over the past five years. But I can't complain, I make so much more money and have such better job security, then the majority of the families I teach. I see first-hand what this poverty does: kids go home to empty houses because their parents work long hours. Parents don't have the time or money to sign their kids up for extracurricular activities or help them with homework. Kids turn to gangs and illegal activities. So it turns to us, at the schools, to fix the problem. And if we can stick it out, speak up, look for the good...maybe things will get better. They have to.

From: TeacherAmanda@hometownmail.com
To: TeacherMaria@hometownmail.com
Subject: RE: Edit?
September 15 at 3:15 PM

Go get 'em girl! This is so spot on, keep it just how it is. Unless maybe you want to call out Dr. Sputnik and how she doesn't help us with anything unless it involves filling out paperwork to send to the state? Ha! No, this is perfect, send it in.

They'd be crazy not to publish it. Who knew you had such a voice, maybe you should run for union president?

Hey, this weekend is Winston's show - do you and the girls want to go?

That was it. That was my selfish response. She was reaching out to me and I just flipped her back a cheery response. She was begging for help! And three days later she was dead. Even after all this time, all the psychiatric sessions, my guilt hasn't really gone away. Even if logically I know there was nothing I could have done.

Day 29

Day 29

I am well. Much, much better. Healthy and free of any dependency issues. Some vitamins and herbs (Melatonin and Vitamin B, Fish Oil) to help me sleep. No alcohol or anything else that might mess me up. Yes, the pain of saying goodbye to my dear friend still hurts. The old hurts from lost relationships and struggles to raise my children alone still hits me in the chest. The stress of my job still remains. But at least now I can feel the pain and I am healing.

I have clean cupboards, an organized garage, pretty bedrooms, clear shelves, closets where we can actually see the floors. I'm clear-headed and calm, no tears or moping. Sleeping pretty well. But - I'm supposed to go back on Monday and at first the administrators were very vague and noncommittal about how or where or even whether a second doctor's note will be sufficient evidence that I am "fit to return". After arriving late to our meeting that they had scheduled three weeks ago, both hemmed and hawed about my fate. The union representative kept asking but they said they need another doctor's note, this one was not sufficient. And they especially didn't like how the doctor suggested I go back only part time (no more last class of the day issues!!!!) I felt like they were saying I return full time or else I can't come back at all. But then they seemed to forget they want me back full time when they ask am I well? Am I safe? Are kids safe? Am I still on medication? That last one was hard to answer calmly. Do they have any idea how many teachers are on anti-depressants? Or just how many people in general? When did taking medication for depression (or anything else) become a possible reason not to let someone do their job?

They finally ended with, "Well…you can start Monday, but we want to make sure you are in a good position. Would having a teaching assistant help you?"

Would it? WOULD it? An assistant? I could hardly believe it! I nodded and said thank you wondering if maybe they want to help me after all. They were quick to let me know it would only be two periods a day…but…a TEACHING ASSISTANT!!! Administrators usually reserve extra help for their friends. Yes!! The union president gave me a smile and I could tell she was happy for me too.

Now I am calm. I'm ready to go back. I feel very free and light about the whole thing. Because…today life is good. Despite job fluctuations and uncertainty. Despite losing Maria. Despite my struggles with Will or with Sonara or Dex. Life is good and I have to look for it. I love my family so much, thank goodness for Winston, and Cody, and Sam. For Carlisle. My parents and brother. Thank goodness for our comfortable home. My beautiful hometown. New and old friends. Opportunities. Upcoming good times - travel, parties, good food. Love and friendship and connections.

Day 30

Day 30

An ironic twist would be so great here. I return to work and a student bursts in and shoots me and a bunch of other students. Then while I'm recovering from my gunshot wound Carlisle gets in a car wreck and dies. I flip out again in grief so I get fired from my job because they view me as mentally unstable. Homeless, I have to live in Dex's backyard in a tent with my boys, watching enviously as he and Sonara live the life I thought for awhile that I wanted. Will finds out I'm homeless and sues me for custody and wins, taking my boys from me. I end up turning to heroin like Jim, eventually dying of an overdose.

….or I could just get a nice reprieve for awhile. Content to hug my boys and my love. Happy to have a job where I can help people and earn enough money for my own home. Glad to be thankful for a beautiful life and glad to enjoy it for one more day.

Megan McArther lives in a small town in the Pacific Northwest with her family. Besides writing she enjoys knitting, yoga, and kayaking. When she has time, Megan plays the drums and rides her large motorcycle.

For more information on her latest projects and to sign up for her mailing list, visit platformpublishers.com

www.ingramcontent.com/pod-product-compliance
Lightning Source LLC
Chambersburg PA
CBHW021446240626
47153CB00001B/320